Canadian Biography Series

GABRIELLE ROY:
CREATION AND MEMORY

A portrait of Gabrielle Roy taken in the fall of 1944.

Gabrielle Roy

CREATION AND MEMORY

Linda M. Clemente
and
William A. Clemente

ECW PRESS

CANADIAN CATALOGUING IN PUBLICATION DATA

Clemente, Linda M., 1950–
Gabrielle Roy : Creation and memory

ISBN 1-55022-287-2

1. Roy, Gabrielle, 1909–1983 – Biography.
2. Authors, Canadian (French) – 20th century –
Biography.* I. Clemente, William A. II. Title.

PS8535.095Z63 1997   C843'.54   C96-931396-9
PQ3919.R74Z63 1997

This book has been published with the assistance of grants
from The Canada Council and the Ontario Arts Council.

Design and imaging by ECW Type & Art, Oakville, Ontario.
Printed by Imprimerie Gagné Ltée, Louiseville, Quebec.

Distributed by General Distribution Services,
30 Lesmill Road, Don Mills, Ontario M3B 2T6.
(416) 445-3333, (800) 387-0172 (Canada), FAX (416) 445-5967.

Distributed in the United Kingdom by Cardiff Academic Press,
St. Fagans Road, Fairwater, Cardiff, Wales, CF5 3AE.

Published by ECW PRESS,
2120 Queen Street East, Suite 200
Toronto, Ontario M4E 1E2.

http://www.ecw.ca/press

ACKNOWLEDGEMENTS

Others helped to bring this book to fruition. We are grateful to Charlotte Burr, Librarian at Ripon College's Lane Library, for jump-starting our thinking with numerous computer searches. For the subsequent acquisition of materials, we are indebted to Don Shankman, Library Technician at the Ripon College Library. His painstaking efforts to obtain even the most arcane materials led to our encounter via e-mail with Lorna Knight, Chief of the Canadian Literature Research Service at the National Library of Canada in Ottawa. Lorna made easy what seemed, for awhile, an obscure task: obtaining pictures of Gabrielle Roy. François Ricard, a noted authority on Gabrielle Roy and one of the executors of her estate, gave us the necessary permissions to include these photographs. On the other side of Canada in Roy's hometown, Alfred Fortier and Angèle Chaput of La Société historique de Saint-Boniface, in the light of expiring deadlines, dispatched even more photographs and permissions. Vida Vande Slunt, Secretary at Ripon College, proofread and printed our final manuscript, her famous smile providing encouragement. Jennifer Schank, Student Assistant at Ripon's Department of Romance and Classical Languages, photocopied the original sources for our citations, a thankless task she undertook meticulously.

On a personal note, our children deserve many presents for not disowning us during the hot, wretchedly humid summer days that accompanied the final stretches of writing. We owe no one more, however, than Libby Glenn, mother and mother-in-law. She arrived when she was needed the most, took a crash course in computers, and polished the last third of our manuscript. The final paragraphs will remain special to the three of us: Bill provided their genesis long distance over the phone, Libby brought them to maturity from hastily scrawled notes, and Linda adjusted word choice to ensure that the closing thoughts resonate our understanding of the gifted writer, Gabrielle Roy.

PHOTOGRAPHS: Cover photo, © National Library of Canada, is used by permission of the Fonds Gabrielle Roy et Fonds Roy-Carbotte, Literary Manuscript Collection, National Library of Canada, NL 17533; frontispiece illustration, 1944, © Annette and Basil Zarov, is used by permission of Basil Zarov and the Fonds Gabrielle Roy et Fonds Roy-Carbotte, Literary Manuscript Collection, National Library of Canada, NL 18236; illustration 2, 1945, © Annette and Basil Zarov, is used by permission of Basil Zarov and the Fonds Gabrielle Roy et Fonds Roy-Carbotte, Literary Manuscript Collection, National Library of Canada, NL 18349; illustration 3, [c. 1943], is used by permission of the Fonds Gabrielle Roy et Fonds Roy-Carbotte, Literary Manuscript Collection, National Library of Canada, NL 18614; illustration 4, 1948, © National Library of Canada, is used by permission of the Fonds Gabrielle Roy et Fonds Roy-Carbotte, Literary Manuscript Collection, National Library of Canada,

Dedicated to
Libby and Betty

TABLE OF CONTENTS

LIST OF ILLUSTRATIONS

Gabrielle Roy

CREATION AND MEMORY

THE JOURNEY OUT

On a fall day in 1937, a twenty-eight-year-old elementary school teacher from the small French-speaking prairie town of Saint-Boniface nervously boarded a train in Winnipeg, Manitoba. Her destination was not, as might be imagined, Quebec, the centre of French Canadian heritage and culture, and her parents' home province. Although she had given serious thought to such a move and would, in a few years, make a home of Quebec for the rest of her life, a recent summer stay there had "convinced her otherwise — she found it an insular place whose inhabitants made her feel like an outsider" (Manitoba Heritage Council 7). Instead, her itinerary came to include Paris, London, and Provence. Her ostensible reason for travelling to Europe was to take drama classes, to perfect the requisite talents for a successful career on the stage or, if not that, at least to enhance her teaching and amateur acting abilities. Her actual motivation, however, she simply could not articulate at this juncture in her life: "I had no definite ideas in mind," she would say to an interviewer almost fifty years later. "I only know that I felt a strong need to travel, to see the world that existed outside of

Canada" (Delson-Karan 196). This young woman was responding to an inner voice compelling her to escape — perhaps even to forsake — the increasingly confining rural environment of the Manitoba plains, a place to which she would eventually return frequently and happily, but only in her imagination. Through her future fiction about life on the Canadian prairies, she would seek to accomplish, in significant ways, the task common to all her relatives who had settled what her grandmother called the "barbarian lands" of Manitoba: "recreating what they had left behind" (Roy, *Fragile* 145).

This brave woman, driven by something ill-defined to search for something unknown, was, of course, Gabrielle Roy, one of Canada's and Quebec's premier authors. In retrospect, her departure from Winnipeg in 1937 denotes a significant transition in her life.

Given the well-trod trails blazed throughout Europe since the 1960s by young and often cocksure adults outfitted with backpacks, armed with ample traveller's cheques, and buoyed up by the parental safety net of a credit card, and given, moreover, the Me Generation's current parlance of needing "space" in which to "find oneself," hitting the road in search of adventure may well strike the modern reader as clichéd. Taking into consideration, however, the closed nature of Saint-Boniface's small Francophone community in the 1930s and its less than enthusiastic acceptance of change, especially regarding traditional gender roles, Gabrielle Roy's determination to pull up roots and cast herself adrift at the height of the Great Depression reveals not whimsy but courage. That she had managed to save approximately $800 from her meagre teacher's salary of less than $100 a month, while supporting both herself and her mother, affirms as well that she made no split-second decision to leave. She had been planning a dramatic change for some time. The decision, however, came as a shock to nearly everyone. "As far as anyone could see, Gabrielle's life was all it should have been," explains Joan Hind-Smith. "Young girls at that time did not suddenly just pack up and go to Europe — certainly not to study drama, of

FIGURE 2

An official portrait of Gabrielle Roy after the overnight success of her first novel, The Tin Flute *(Bonheur d'occasion), in 1945. Roy is thirty-six years old.*

all things. During the Depression anyone with a job was lucky just to be drawing a salary, and here was Gabrielle, trying to outreach herself as usual" (77). For a woman to undertake this uncertain journey alone against both societal and parental opposition — most, including her mother, thought that quitting a job when so few people had work bordered on the insane — underscores not only this unique individual's resolve but also her strength in coping with the emotional assaults of a guilty conscience and painful alienation. Indeed, she was hurt a great deal by the adverse reaction from those around her. Of all this stubborn young woman's relatives, only her cloistered sister, Bernadette, supported her decision, and for the rest of her life, Gabrielle remained grateful.

After the ups and downs of her two-year stay in Europe and on the eve of World War II in 1939, Gabrielle Roy quit London and sailed to Montreal with the few dollars remaining from her travels and from her aborted attempts at education. Alone and desperate for money, Roy decided not to return "home," where her former teaching position at the Académie Provencher was being held open and where her mother, Mélina Roy, anxiously awaited her, but instead to devote her energies fully to the uncertain vocation of writing, a decision her friends and family found more ridiculous than her cavalier flight from Saint-Boniface. As Betty Bednarski writes concerning this consequential decision, "To break free (from family, from inward-looking community) was the dominant impulse as Roy set out for Europe from Manitoba. To *stay* free was her one overriding concern two years later as she made the decision, in spite of her mother's expectations, to remain in Montreal" (29). Did Roy make the right decision by staying in Montreal? Instant international fame and immediate acclaim for her first novel, *The Tin Flute* (*Bonheur d'occasion*), published six years later, answers that question with a resounding "Yes!"

In retrospect, readers encountering the array of memorable characters in her work must wonder where those characters originated, especially since Roy's first thirty years of experience, aside from a few adventures in Europe, were confined largely to life in Manitoba's isolated and seemingly uneventful French-speaking communities. Certainly, however, her own background as part of a disenfranchised and economically disadvantaged minority surrounded by and dependent on the English-speaking world — instilling a worldview that was later reinforced during her long walks through the impoverished Saint-Henri district of Montreal — accounts in part for her gripping portrayals of Rose-Anna, Florentine, and the uncompromising Jean Lévesque in *The Tin Flute*. What she writes about Saint-Boniface in *The Fragile Lights of Earth* holds true for the oppressed community depicted in her first novel: "Saint-Boniface breathed, prayed, hoped, sang and suffered in French, but it earned its living in English, in the offices, stores and factories of Winnipeg. The irremediable and existential difficulty of being French-Canadian in Manitoba or elsewhere!" (150). And recollections gleaned from a summer teaching position (taken for the salary of five dollars a day to bolster savings for her European adventures) in the Water Hen region of northern Manitoba, coupled with several pivotal experiences as the beneficiary of other people's generosity, help explain such unforgettable creations as Luzina Tousignant and Father Joseph-Marie (a Capuchin monk whose parish, Toutes-Aides, is synonymous with his capabilities) in *Where Nests the Water Hen*. Roy's early years in Saint-Boniface likewise account, in part, for Christine and the numerous other vivid characters who populate the stories collected in *Street of Riches* and *The Road Past Altamont*, narratives M.G. Hesse treats together in a chapter entitled "A Pilgrimage to the Past." For a number of years, moreover, Roy taught young immigrant children, and these memories form the stage on which the six children spotlighted in *Children of My Heart* perform. In a similar fashion, the neighbours and friends gathered in *Enchanted Summer* spring from Roy's holidays spent at her summer home, and from a visit there by her dear sister Bernadette, in the county of Charlevoix, some sixty miles north of Quebec City.

But what chords from Roy's seemingly tranquil life vibrate in the lonely, haunted painter Pierre Cadorai, the protagonist of *The Hidden Mountain*; in the dainty, ageing, magical Eveline of *De quoi t'ennuies-tu, Eveline?*; in the eponymous Alexandre Chenevert (protagonist of her second novel, published in English as *The Cashier*), whose pathetic, frail shoulders bear too many of the world's burdens? While writing *Windflower*, a collection of three short stories and a novella about the invasion of the Arctic world by the supposedly superior white civilization, from what source did Roy draw for the sensitive delineation of Elsa's battles as the Eskimo mother of a Métis son? And what experience accounts for the vagabond Sam Lee Wong, the mystic Doukhobors, and Martha and her garden in *Garden in the Wind*? What, finally, is the story of Gabrielle Roy, a woman who, after the publication of her multiple-prize-winning first novel in 1945, essentially retired from the public sphere by choice to protect herself not only from the anxieties and tensions attendant upon fame but also, and simply, from daily existence? Although Ringuet's remark prefacing a short interview with Roy, published in 1951, is certainly a bit exaggerated, he captures an essential feature of the author's persona: "I never knew a person more secretive or more of an enemy to herself" (our translation). Partial responses to some of the preceding questions, as well as significant insights into this remarkable woman's character, can be gleaned from an examination of Roy's life during her two-year sojourn in Europe. Before turning to the years prior to her departure and her later years as a professional writer, we want first to consider this transitional period. Of singular significance for her life is the fact that during this breathing space from Canada, Gabrielle Roy became a writer.

PARIS, CITY OF LIGHT

Gabrielle Roy's first two weeks in Paris, the famous City of Light — Montmartre, Gertrude Stein, Hemingway, Picasso, Ezra Pound, Place Pigalle, the Comédie Française, the Eiffel Tower, Notre Dame, the Métro, a city to benefit from or to be damned in — proved less than auspicious. Roy recalls many of the painful details in her autobiography, *Enchantment and Sorrow*. Her first mistake was simply to arrive at her boarding-house, Mme Jouve's on the rue de la Santé, with an oversized trunk, which her landlady immediately consigned to the base-ment, located, it seemed to Roy, in the bowels of Paris. Her second error followed closely: when offered something to drink before going to bed, she pictured her mother's steaming hot chocolate but accepted instead a lemonade, knowing well the physical consequences for her. Her ensuing third misstep: responding to nature's call every fifteen minutes, she flushed after *every* use, unleashing a cacophonous avalanche of water. It was only the following morning that she realized that her behaviour, intended as good manners, bordered on folly, for the noise most certainly awakened everybody, probably even the concierge six floors below. Thus, her attempts to be a sophisticated city dweller only caused embarrassment.

Thanks to the assistance of a young Canadian woman studying and working as an au pair in Paris, Roy slowly became somewhat better acclimatized. The young woman, who had been contacted by a mutual acquaintance, found a boarding-house, met Roy at the train station, and showed her around Paris. But after approximately two weeks of this new and chaotic environment, her coping skills exhausted, Roy retreated to her room. Thus far into her frustrating stay, Roy's only real moment of well-being had occurred while dining at her friend's tiny but cosy top-floor apartment, naturally lit by a large skylight. After dinner, the two young women stood tiptoe on chairs to view the Paris that captures the hearts of so many. In contrast to the vistas afforded by such well-known places as Notre Dame, the Sacré Coeur, the Eiffel Tower, and, nowadays, la Défense, the skylight view of Paris was far more intimate. As would happen frequently in her life, a humble place offered respite. Her other respite lay in her imagination.

In an attempt to draw Roy out, Mme Jouve gave her Alain-Fournier's *Le grand Meaulnes*, a novel then adored by all Paris; however, the young Canadian's unfavourable reaction disap-pointed her hostess. Compared with Roy's own capacity for fantasizing, that of the hero struck her as rather tame. Indeed, instead of the sensitive lad's longing for someone who turned out to be not too far away in actual time and distance, Roy's imaginative escape transported her from the impersonal urban bustle of Paris to the beautiful pastoral surroundings of the Little Water Hen, to a time of ineffable tranquillity and harmony. Although she had no way of knowing at the time, these two places of enchantment — her friend's tiny room and northern Manitoba — would reappear, filtered through the double sieve of art and experience, in her fiction as Pierre Cadorai's skylit Paris apartment in *The Hidden Mountain* and as the setting for her favourite work, *Where Nests the Water Hen*, that place where, she muses, "if they wished, men could perhaps make a fresh start" (*Fragile* 189).

In the meantime, however, she had Paris and unfulfilled hopes with which to contend. Eventually, remembering that she had ventured there to study theatre, Roy dutifully attended a few plays — productions which, although later in life she grew to admire French theatre, left her cold. The French manner of interpreting the works of great writers such as Giraudoux, Racine, and Rostand (*Cyrano de Bergerac*) struck her as contrived, as overwrought. Even the famous actor Louis Jouvet — distinguished also as a director, especially for his productions of Molière and Giraudoux — failed to move her; she found his delivery "cold and flat," his acting mere "face-pulling" (*Enchantment* 217). All of which left her mentally in disarray. Buttressed with little more than great expectations, she had sacrificed home, job, and family to study acting in Paris, only to discover suddenly, at least for the moment, that what she really did *not* want to do was study acting in Paris! Her reaction was to hit the streets of Paris, endlessly and aimlessly walking, walking, walking, upbraiding herself, wallowing in indecision and, doubtless, self-pity.

Distressed at her young Canadian's behaviour, Mme Jouve did her best to help. Thanks to an appointment made by her landlady, who had some remarkable connections, Roy appeared one fateful afternoon at L'Atelier to explore the possibility of studying under Charles Dullin, director and founder of this successful theatre and a man of considerable stature known internationally for his innovative productions of classical and modern drama. She arrived in a darkened theatre only to interrupt a rehearsal of Ben Jonson's *Volpone*. Dullin's scowling countenance, his apparently ugly, crippled body, and his decision to interview her by shouting condescending questions from the stage so unnerved the future award-winning author that when literally saved by the bell — in this case, a telephone call for the imposing M. Dullin — Gabrielle Roy determined to exit stage left: she fled.

Her misery and her purposelessness now confirmed, Roy again took to the Parisian sidewalks, putting one foot in front of the other and feeling deeply isolated from the humanity surrounding her. And yet she walked nevertheless with some purpose. As it turned out, during these numerous lonely sidewalk strolls through this city of marvels, Roy absorbed bits and pieces of the world around her, though unaware how useful this material would eventually prove. Once tapped, her facility for recalling vivid details opened floodgates that made her realize, but only years later, the long-dormant importance these lonely walks held. As she writes in her autobiography, "In the long run wasting time has often proved to be its most profitable use for me, but I wasn't conscious of this . . . yet and kept berating myself bitterly" (*Enchantment* 222). A nice justification, certainly, for not putting time to other use; however, while some unknown force besides fear alone propelled her from Dullin's theatre and perhaps saved her from a career that did not suit her, Roy still found herself in Paris with limited funds, supposedly trying to uncover her destiny, and, like most of us, she still felt accountable for her actions.

Was the theatre still her destination, but perhaps in a different guise? Roy certainly thought so the day one of her peregrinations led her to a small theatre where the sorrowful eyes of Ludmilla Pitoëff, gazing from the playbill announcing Chekhov's *The Seagull*, arrested the young woman's desultory wandering and invited her in to watch the performance.

Having always admired Chekhov's short stories, Roy was even more enchanted to see his play laying bare the loneliness, bewilderment, and misunderstandings of ordinary people through the gifted talents of George and Ludmilla Pitoëff. For Roy, the import of this experience was twofold. Her immediate response was to write an impassioned letter to Ludmilla Pitoëff, in which she both poured out her admiration of the actor's talent and chronicled her own confusion and uncertainty (a letter not unlike those Gabrielle Roy would later receive from young writers looking for similar direction and advice). The other effect of Chekhov à la Pitoëff was the immediate and long-lasting affinity Roy felt for humble, unassuming places and thus for the humble, unassuming people who inhabit them. Chekhov's penchant for telling the truth about the human condition via the men and women who are usually lost in a crowd, as well as his disdain for artful tricks, illusion, or even lies, anticipate Roy's oeuvre. As she often repeated in interviews up to the time of her death, "I have always greatly admired *La Steppe* by Chekhov. This work was the one that inspired me to blend my characters into the environment from which they came" (Delson-Karan 199). This insistence on writing the truth, thorny, irreverent, and mercurial as it may be — and Gabrielle Roy would be the first to admit its elusiveness — nevertheless permeates her works in her attempt to unveil for her readers aspects of the everyday conditions that touch us all. To this end, the concluding lines of the essay she prepared for *Man and His World* (*Terre des hommes*), a collection of photographs for Expo '67 commissioned by the Canadian government, not only give voice to that particular world fair's theme of optimism but also beautifully articulate a stubborn hope that informs much of her life's work:

Perhaps we are nearly there. . . .
Are we not there when we give voice to the simplest and most just expression of the heart? When that heart can open up in confidence rather than shrink in revolt?

When it no longer refuses to recognize itself in the criminal, as it so easily identifies with the hero? *Terre des hommes*, it seems to me *happens* every time we succeed in putting ourselves in the place of others. (*Fragile* 222)

The frustrations that initially goaded Roy in Paris eventually forced her to make important decisions, but she did not make them overnight. In making major decisions, we are often confronted by closed doors. Given life's capriciousness, a portal that opens without effort is often suspect, while one that initially resists attempts to pry it open may eventually reveal a path to great rewards. Roy's letter to Ludmilla Pitoëff opened a door with little effort. Roy arrived back at Mme Jouve's one day to find her landlady in an excited state, for the famous actor's secretary had telephoned not once but twice, inviting Roy to the theatre to meet Mme Pitoëff. Their subsequent meeting, which initially promised much and rekindled the amateur actor from Saint-Boniface's interest in the stage, eventually resulted only in an open invitation to attend rehearsals — which Roy did. Soon, however, she missed one, a couple of days later another, and finally she stopped going altogether. The contrived nature of actors in street clothes searching for their characters, the failure of ropes, pulleys, and other backstage paraphernalia to embody the magic they create in an actual performance, and the boredom of sitting with little to do amidst deserted seats all combined to distress her. She preferred real life, sitting in parks and cafés, walking, and observing — but to what end? This dramatic education, which had so much to do with her becoming an outstanding writer, only depressed her, compounding the misery of not having definite direction.

Despite the angst that afflicted Gabrielle Roy in her quest to discover both herself and her calling, being a traveller allowed her the delicious freedom to pack up and leave an inhospitable place or otherwise unfruitful situation. And so she did. While France might seem the natural place to nurture the development of a French Canadian intensely loyal to and proud of her ancestral heritage and language, happy memories of a few days in London prior to her arrival in Paris, squired around by a friend from Winnipeg, drew her out of her funk and back across the English Channel. Later in life, she would return to France and experience some happy times, but for now it was England that provided this directionless young woman with necessary direction.

LONDON CALLING

Roy's tendency toward inertia consumed her first fortnight in London. Her friend Bohdan Hubicki from Winnipeg, a violinist studying at the Royal Academy of Music, had found her lodgings on Wickendon Street, in the working-class district of Fulham. But renting a cold room from dour automatons in what seemed the grand city's most silent house did not bode well, for combined with London's then famous fog, this locale only exacerbated Roy's lethargy. Whether it was the intensity of her non-activity that finally sparked her to action, or merely her youth taking its turn, or perhaps a capacity, inherited from her mother, to rebound from adversity into sunshine, Roy's torpor eventually gave way to momentum: she visited Piccadilly Circus, attended the theatre, moved to a happier room above Geoffrey Price's Bicycle and Radio Repair Shop in a busier, livelier, and eminently more cheerful neighbourhood, and enrolled at the Guildhall School of Music and Drama. Gabrielle came alive, her improved mood having, moreover, regenerated for a time the original enthusiasm for the stage that recent experiences in Paris had dampened. Thus, despite the not insignificant cost of enrolment, payable up front in cash, and despite having to devote efforts to more than just acting and studying the plays themselves — the complete course included makeup, fencing, and tap dancing — Roy still nursed the vague calling of a career onstage. She went so far as to enrol as well in a French drama course with Mme Gachet, tutor to such notables as Vivien Leigh and Charles Laughton.

The seriousness of her renewed interest in her "calling" not-withstanding, her walks around the city, particularly those that took her along the Thames, brought her the most happiness. She also came to know London by riding the upper decks of buses, sometimes to the end of the line and back again. Roy would likewise familiarize herself with Montreal by streetcar when she settled there in 1939, just as her penchant for long walks anticipated a lifelong habit.

Although one might think that living off funds with no possibility of replenishment would force Roy to take full advantage of her time and costly education in London, Roy later remembered her dreaming along the Thames, on the upper decks of the bright red London buses, and at the landlady's cabin opposite Hampton Court as more real and sustaining than anything she experienced at Guildhall. The writer-in-the-making seems so apparent with hindsight; yet her aptitude for writing remained dormant, and her discouragement with any sentences she had attempted in the past convinced her that her talents lay in some other area. Besides, her experiences at Guildhall were not without reward, just as she was hardly without talent. Once, while reading Portia's emotional plea to the judge in Shakespeare's *The Merchant of Venice* in front of her classmates and forgetting herself as the woes of her own childhood transformed her performance, Roy astounded her listeners to silence; the spectacle left them dumbfounded, moved not only by her interpretation but also by the depth of tragic strains from a woman best known to them for her gaiety. Impressed by the young woman's performance, Roy's teacher, Miss Rorke (a name immortalized in the jingoistic, Anglophone spinster Miss O'Rorke in *Where Nests the Water Hen*), notable for her acerbity and alacrity when reminding students of their incompetence, offered free tutoring to her gifted student during evening hours. Roy availed herself of the opportunity two or three times, until giving up on the "witch, which, wither, whither, wisht, whished, whim, whichever" (*Enchantment* 259–60). One day while she studied Racine with Mme Gachet, the irascible instructor hurled a book at Roy's head, publicly confirming her ineptitude in comprehending seventeenth-century French drama and further injuring her always fragile confidence.

Although Gabrielle Roy obviously endured an anguished search for self-identity and a profession, the cheerful side of her nature would, at times, prevail. Her autobiography, interviewers, and friends attest to Roy's gaiety, to her delightful sense of humour, and to the enthusiasm that often caused her to jump up in the middle of a narration to act out comically a character or to add dramatic effect. As Joyce Marshall says of her good friend, Roy "possessed great energy and could *on occasion* be very funny, . . . holding a room spellbound or shaking with laughter — *provided the room was not too crowded and contained only her friends*" (36; our emphasis). Her loneliness and depression notwithstanding, Roy remained resilient; with a natural bent toward self-effacement, she could step back and find humour in her moments of self-doubt and self-pity, even bringing cheer and laughter to those around her.

This complex personality, constrained by poverty and family ties in her youth and by the confining role of virgin schoolmarm throughout her twenties, blossomed in Europe and was not without its admirers. Her first memorable beau, a tall, dark, handsome Welshman, happened to hear Roy's reading of Portia's plea that one special day and took tea with her, much to the envy of her female classmates. Roy did not know at the time that her companion was currently one of England's finest baritones who sang often at Covent Garden and was familiar to listeners of the BBC. His talent and fame, however, missed their mark with Gabrielle Roy, for his self-assurance and grand ways obscured the qualities that might otherwise have attracted her: his humble background as a coal miner's son and as a miner himself. Although often in the clouds when dreaming of her future endeavours, Roy so far had her feet firmly planted on the ground in terms of romance. In her youth, during summers at her beloved Uncle Excide's farm, Roy breached many of the rules of country courtship when it came to gentlemen callers. In fact, she had difficulty suppressing laughter in the presence of the young bumbling bumpkins who stared at her wistfully while singing western tunes that moved Gabrielle not.

At those awkward moments, Roy must have sensed that her destiny was to become someone other than a small-town, spinster teacher or country wife. Nor did the opposite extreme — becoming the wife of a famous Welsh baritone — capture her imagination or interest. He did escort her once to a reception at the Austrian embassy, he impressive in gentlemen's evening attire complete with a top hat, a gold-headed cane, and a black velvet cape that swept the ground. Roy, equal to the occasion, wore a bright red taffeta dress with matching shoes, her hair done up in ringlets. End of story, however, for the glamorous singer failed to sweep her off her feet.

Similarly, no sparks flew between Roy and Bohdan, her close and helpful friend from Winnipeg. Although not yet as famous as the flamboyant baritone, the much gentler Bohdan also devoted himself to a career in music. Driven by more identifiable demons than Roy, Bohdan nevertheless pursued the more difficult road. Having left Canada with no more than his violin, he worked off his passage labouring on a cattle boat to London. Once arrived, he took odd jobs at night so he could practise Bach during the day or spend his scarce savings on sporadic lessons with the best violin teachers in London. He also sacrificed his health for this foremost love of his life. After a year in London and coincidental with Gabrielle's arrival from Paris, Bohdan was on the point of signing a contract with the BBC for a weekly program. Within a few weeks after her arrival, he played at the Royal Albert Hall to the acclaim of the London music world. Roy attended that performance, and after witnessing the intensity of his passion for the violin, she understood why their friendship could never have blossomed into romance. Both driven by their individual imperatives, his evident and hers inchoate on the horizon, neither Bohdan nor Gabrielle would have the requisite room in their lives for the equally intense and consuming demands of romance.

Yet Bohdan nevertheless formed a curious part in Roy's life. Among other things, he found her her first lodgings in London, he helped her move to her new room above the bicycle shop, he left her occasional theatre tickets, and, significantly enough, he confidently and accurately envisioned her future. Ever since they had met five or six years earlier back in Winnipeg, Bohdan had predicted that Roy would become a famous writer. While his vision of his own future was clouded and stretched ahead only a few years, he claimed to see very clearly Gabrielle Roy's name in big letters, not on the marquee of a theatre, but on the cover of a book. As a consequence, he had initially chosen the quiet room on Wickendon Street in the working-class district of Fulham for Roy to live in, assured that the tranquillity, rather than stifle her, would favour her writing. In her autobiography, Roy fondly recounts how Bohdan, pretending to read the tea leaves in the bottom of her cup, foretold of her writing "an earthy, populist novel, which wouldn't really be surprising, since [she] felt so much at home with working people" (*Enchantment* 254). As surely as her prescient friend could not predict his own future — and for good reason, for Bohdan died during the war when a German bomb exploded over the house in which he lived — he foresaw Roy's remarkable success. His was a supportive voice, not only in London but also earlier in Canada when others had sharply criticized Gabrielle's early experiments in creative writing. More immediately, he had met the man he predicted would steal her heart.

ENCHANTMENT AND SORROW

After a proper introduction, thanks to Bohdan, Lady Frances Ryder of Cadogan Gardens in South Kensington welcomed Roy at her teatime gatherings, open to students of all colours from all corners of the British Empire. For many students, Lady Frances's teas offered them their best meal of the week. In addition to food, Lady Frances and those of her ilk also handed out theatre, ballet, or concert tickets, as well as invitations to stay as a guest in stately homes, often in Wales or even Ireland. Roy would eventually accept a couple of these invitations, but her shyness, coupled with her previous experience of the snobbish wealthy Anglophones in Winnipeg, was such that rubbing shoulders with the landed gentry in England lacked the lustre it held for other students. Several male students in this group did single out Roy for particular attention. One of them, a New Zealander named David, even invited her to join him and his mother for a ten-day tour around southern England. At the same time that Roy delighted in the silence, the peacefulness, and the alluring natural beauty of Devon, Cornwall, Gloucestershire, the Moors, and the countless and beautiful unnamed little villages throughout the countryside, David and his mother sized her up as a potential member of their family. In the end, the two must have found her wanting in some way and consequently labelled her "unsuitable" because David's attentions thereafter waned and finally stopped completely. The dismissal of David as "not very good value" by a certain Lady Wells, however, confirmed Roy's own sense of what lay beneath his reserved, polite manner, with his too too impeccably British voice and his umbrella rolled oh-so-tight (*Enchantment* 275). Roy yearned instead for warmth, passion, a kindred soul, a this-can-only-happen-in-the-movies love, and this period in her life, as it turned out, was the only one that allowed the time such a love demands.

And it happened, following a script right out of the movies: she arrived one afternoon at Lady Frances's and there he sat, a stranger across a crowded room, his dark eyes drawing her closer as Lady Wells shepherded her to his table, coincidentally intent on her meeting this someone really special. Surprised, undone, astonished, afraid it was all a dream, they remained speechless, gazing at each other, wonder-struck, magnetized, energized. Once on their own, the doors of Lady Frances's home closed behind them, they walked, fingers enlaced, in no particular direction. Romantic love, with all its irrational fears, anxieties, and joys, suddenly crowded everything else out of Gabrielle Roy's life. Love, in this case named Stephen, became her beacon. And for a few idyllic and memorable months, Roy came to believe the impossible possible: enchantment without sorrow.

Of course, enchantment without sorrow can only ever be ephemeral, more substantive in imagination than in actual practice. Moreover, as Roy affirms throughout her oeuvre, enchantment and sorrow tend more to be concomitant than mutually exclusive. To Donald Cameron she explained the marriage between tears and joy that she seeks to establish in her writing: "I have no sooner seen the splendour of life than I feel obliged, physically obliged, to look down and also take notice of the sad and of the tragic in life" (131). And so it was for her during those fervent, love-filled months that she and Stephen shared, ephemeral to be sure, but grand for a time. Upon taking her home after that first heady afternoon and evening together, rather than kiss her good-bye, Stephen laid his head on her shoulder, a gesture she wistfully interpreted as an expression of the refuge he had found in her. Such a token of trust moved her emotionally as much as his touch electrified her — she was, in a word, smitten. As might be imagined, they quickly became inseparable, doubting the other's existence until they saw each other again. Time away from the other was an eternity of anguish, a hell to be endured, hours or days wasted until they could be together again. All these common symptoms were suffered by a woman who, tender as her sense of romantic love was, had been kept from it by her fear of love, certain that it was rarely happy, that you really could never recover what it consumed of you, that it was irreversible and, in the end, always painful. One recalls Christine's reaction, in "To Prevent a Marriage," a story from Street of Riches, to her elder sister Georgianna's protestations about loving the man her parents argue against her marrying: "Afterward, almost always throughout my life, I have been unable to hear a human being say, 'I love . . .' without feeling my heart contract with fear, and wanting with both my arms to clasp that so sadly vulnerable being and protect it" (44). Despite her fears, however, Roy yearned irresistibly for what true love also ideally promised: unadulterated happiness. And so, at twenty-nine, for the first time and for the last time, she gave herself completely to a man whose feverish, tumultuous, possessive love held her in its thrall.

Stephen and Gabrielle were happy — happy when together, at least. When apart, Gabrielle's love for Stephen so consumed her thoughts that the passion isolated her from the world around her, a world essential to the author within. In truth, this intense attraction was doomed from the moment the outside world, of necessity, intruded. Then imagination confronted the always ambivalent world of experience: the shadows of Stalin and Hitler, cast across the Asian and European continents, arrived during the sunshine of a British summer to darken Roy's life. Gabrielle quickly and painfully discovered that Stephen had a secret life and a veiled passion that overruled and circumvented any love he felt for her.

The clairvoyant Bohdan had felt convinced that Gabrielle and Stephen were made for each other. Nevertheless, before Gabrielle met Stephen, Bohdan had confided in her that Stephen was rather enigmatic. Despite their animated and revealing conversations, Bohdan sensed that Stephen tried to obscure the fact that Bohdan actually knew virtually nothing about him. In those infrequent moments when love's turbid waters momentarily cleared, Gabrielle realized indeed that she and Stephen were almost total strangers. He told her only that he was born in Canada of Ukrainian parents and was still a Canadian citizen although he had lived in New York City while attending Columbia University, and that he was currently studying political science at the University of London. After two months of solid companionship, without a word of explanation, Stephen suddenly disappeared from her life for almost a month. Confused, hurt, and anguished, Roy felt her love transform into something akin to distrust. Her keen sense of betrayal after having been so trustingly open with someone saved her from too much victimization and armed her instead for the now inevitable parting of the ways. This alteration in her feelings, however, did not preclude her running to meet Stephen when he finally telephoned, suppressing all her negative feelings and succumbing again to love's powerful dictates. One cannot help but wonder in reviewing Gabrielle Roy's tumultuous first love and later life if the writer in her, though still undefined, reasserted itself during this experience not only to protect her from future relationships of this kind but also to soften its aftermath, for on meeting Stephen again after his unexplained absence, her retrenching began almost immediately. When Stephen slipped his fingers between hers, heretofore a gesture so endearing to her because it felt so natural, that night his touch alarmed her, owing to its now mechanical nature, mechanical not for lack of meaning but from too much experience, perhaps, with other women. Although he knew her well, he was a stranger who had manipulated her. And then, Stephen's explanation for his mysterious departure supplied the coup de grâce to a love already on the wane.

Stephen, it turned out, belonged to a group of Ukrainian militants financed by Ukrainian Americans working toward the overthrow of Soviet domination and toward the independence of the Ukrainian nation, a reality that lay some fifty years in the future. Owing to this region's resistance to the collectivization of agriculture, one of Stalin's pet projects, the Soviet ruler, in what amounts to mass murder, had reduced Ukraine to starvation by engineering one of the worst famines in the region's history. Stephen had committed himself to fight persecution and to avenge Soviet crimes against his people. As such, he worked as a courier of sorts, and his latest trip, he informed Gabrielle, had taken him into a Soviet-dominated country to contact a fellow agent. During that trip, as an example of the constant danger inherent in his life, he had been tailed by the KGB, had hidden in a barn for a week with virtually no food, and was lucky to be back in London at all. His studies at the University of London, he revealed, were only a cover; the driving force in Stephen's life was his political passion. Hardly cognizant of the potential dangers she could face as this man's lover, Gabrielle was hurt by not being first in Stephen's life and then deeply alienated by not being able to share his one true burning passion. That such an overriding concern in his life could have remained hidden during the past months of intimacy, even that one could indeed silence such passion, must have shocked Roy, revealing, among other things, her naïve vulnerability. Certainly her experience with Stephen later coloured her reactions toward Ukrainians living in Canada when she wrote an article for the *Bulletin des agriculteurs* in 1943: "Some," she notes dryly, "are attached to their dream of a free Ukraine, and to these it means more than life or truth" (*Fragile* 81).

The irrationality of one-sided, fervent political commitment is not discussed directly in her autobiography, but the problem would plague Roy for years to come with respect to politics in general and to Quebec politics in particular, just as it had brought her pain in her youth when her father lost his job with the Canadian government, owing to his loyalty to a particular political cause. In the 1930s, money to fund Ukraine's bid for independence came from emigrants who enthusiastically supported the cause. But support also came from Nazi Germany. Hitler, whose armies would devastate Ukraine during the 1941–44 occupation, ensured that the independence movement received what resources he could supply to undermine his nemesis, Stalin. Thus, the independence movement, at least indirectly, aligned itself with Nazi Germany to achieve its ends. Of course, someone like Stephen would rationalize the accusation that he was thus a Nazi sympathizer by claiming that siding with this repressive regime to undermine another equally odious government represented the movement's taking advantage of an opportunity born of necessity. This logic would certainly disturb Roy, who later in life avoided involvement in politics. Passionate political commitment in particular, she observed, "has its dangers":

When you take part in, say, a political crisis, you become — at least *I* become — very very irate, or very ardent, and I begin to see in one direction only. I'm all fire and I'm all injustice, in a sense, because I just take sides so very, very vehemently. (Cameron 135–36)

It is important to note that in her writing and in her actual life, Roy avoided emphatic political commentary just as she eschewed the topic of passionate love, both of which have their dangers.

Despite her feelings of personal betrayal, the relationship with Stephen continued, but at great cost to Gabrielle. Like everyone else, she had to learn a painful lesson: although dealt a mortal blow, love refuses to die instantly. Its continued presence in her life only served to increase the distance between Stephen and her; at the same time, she despised herself for every minute she spent with him and even for the energy she devoted simply to avoid him. But being "out" when he telephoned and returning to her flat later than when she knew he might pass by helped her regain her bearings. During this time, she occupied herself doing . . . nothing. She had more or less abandoned her acting studies, and she saw no one, her disgust with herself having made her more solitary than ever. Devoting herself to purging her life of Stephen created a hiatus of sorts, allowing her not only to evaluate the destructiveness of a relationship such as Stephen and hers but also to give life to the budding writer within. She unconsciously understood that she could never again allow anyone such total domination over her. Stephen's departure for another secret mission at the end of June 1938 gave Gabrielle the room she needed to begin nurturing her future career.

PERFECT STRANGERS

Fortified, perhaps, against love but otherwise drifting from day to day, Roy had only one clear thought: to escape the summer's heat, which had turned her little room into an inferno. To that end, she habitually spent whole days in Trafalgar Square, where, cooled by the huge fountain's spray, she relaxed and took meals at the mobile canteens. One day, for no particular reason other than the pleasure she always took in traversing the boundaries between city and country, Roy boarded a Green Line bus, aptly named for its route, which followed verdant secondary roads up to forty miles outside of London almost into an earlier era of rural villages and cultivated fields.

Roy unwittingly rode the bus to one of the havens that life on occasion steered her toward, a haven in which to renew her strength and to gather momentum. There, as often in her life, she found complete strangers willing, once solicited, to help — very much like Luzina in *Where Nests the Water Hen*, who believes firmly that in times of need even strangers would offer comfort and aid: "Luzina had only to put herself under a human being's protection for him to behave toward her exactly as she wished" (24). In response to the numerous suggestions for potential stopping-off places showered on Roy by passengers and bus driver alike, she decided rather serendipitously to disembark at Wake Arms, a pub closed at the time, to follow an inviting narrow track into the forest. Like the hungry child whose eyes are bigger than her stomach, Roy walked much farther afield than she had anticipated, a trek that left her far too exhausted to retrace her steps. Help was nearby, however, in the form of a thatched-roof cottage, a direct descendant of Tudor England, replete with fragrant delphiniums and hollyhocks, and a sign advertising tea, scones, and crumpets, all served by a hunchbacked young woman named Felicity — none of which could have been better conceived by George Eliot or Thomas Hardy.

So completely relaxed did Roy feel that she fell asleep in her comfortable chair under an arbour. Indeed, life seemed at this place to mirror art. For true to the Romance topos of rebirth, the transition to a new life, here marked by her sleep after a successful voyage down a magic forest path open only to those worthy of the challenge, Roy found herself directed to a night's lodging by her personal oracle, who told her to travel still farther down the path to a place called Century Cottage. Run by Esther Perfect and her aged father, later baptized Father Perfect by Roy, Century Cottage offered the weary traveller a long-sought peace that would allow her to discover and to manifest her burning passion to write.

On the doorstep to Century Cottage, all the cares and anxieties of her short lifetime — poverty, family woes, her lack of direction, a love affair that only aggravated her loneliness — brought tears to Roy's eyes as she collapsed against the doorpost, virtually asleep as her shoulder touched the wood. And in this state she was found by Esther Perfect, Esther whose kind eyes plumbed one's soul, discerning its hurts and anguish. Esther who just a few minutes before had prayed to God to send her one of his creatures to save. As though following the dictates of Providence, Esther led Roy upstairs to the only bedroom in the world that could have suited her at that moment: large; airy; furnished with a big brass bed, washstand, and fireplace; and most important, overlooking the downs from two large windows with white tulle curtains drawn to one side. For the rest of her life, windows — reminiscent of those in the attic in which she found sanctuary as a child and where at ten she had composed a play, a murder mystery, for her friends on Deschambault Street to perform — were imperative to her ability to write. Roy found respite in a way of life reminiscent of Eden, Father Perfect having earned his living as head gardener to the squire on whose estate Century Cottage was located and where he and Esther could remain as long as they lived.

From "Paradise" the London skyline appeared murky, its overcast sky imbued with a kind of insalubrity and desolation. There in Epping Forest, Roy felt protected from unhappiness, confident that it would lie dormant and unhurtful during her stay, although knowing in her heart that the sanctuary could offer only a temporary balm. As Esther herself observed about her father that first night, "He's lived in a kind of Garden of Eden and the woes of mankind haven't touched him as they have most people. And there really isn't much left to say about Eden once the story's been told, is there?" (*Enchantment* 313). Peace. Affection. Rejuvenation. Security. Then departure. Esther, not much more worldly than her father, had nevertheless read a good deal, including *Paradise Lost*, *The Pilgrim's Progress*, the Brontë sisters, Jane Austen, *Gulliver's Travels*, Tennyson, both Brownings, Shakespeare, and the Bible. Esther, Roy soon learned, enjoyed reading daily from Shakespeare as much as from the Bible, finding companionship in these books that expressed better or more completely her own thoughts. Certainly Esther's words were not lost on the writer, Gabrielle Roy, whose special gift was to articulate the thoughts of others and in so doing bring to her readers that special solace only shared feelings can elicit.

Feeling cared for made Roy feel safe, and feeling safe, she found courage. Feeling courage, she rediscovered her confidence in life; feeling the support of those around her, in this case, the Perfects, made her feel obliged to return the favour in the only way she could. The morning following her felicitous arrival at the Perfects' cottage, she had seven or eight pages written by the time Esther entered with the breakfast tray.

With the return in her life of the sense of peace she had experienced during her one summer at the Little Water Hen and her childhood summers at her Uncle Excide's came also the urge and the need to write. As it turned out, Roy always did her best writing in the morning, writing as quickly as possible to catch all the images, ideas, and stories that had germinated during her sleep and awaited her setting pen to paper to bring them to fruition. Although what she wrote that particular morning does not count for much today, she had a keen sense of its being better than anything she'd written before. More important, writing brought her a sense of well-being she had not known for some time. And significantly, the story she wrote that morning came to her in French, ending her vacillation over which language best suited her ideas. As she told Donald Cameron in an interview, writing in English made her serious ideas sound somehow frivolous: "I think a writer speaks from his soul, and your soul is linked to one language more than another, even if you're familiar with several" (130). While she had written in English with some success, the French flowing from her pen that morning awakened her to an identity about which she would no longer have the slightest doubts, delving into her past and drawing strength from her ancestral bonds and the history of her people. Like the youngest Demetrioff in Roy's *Children of My Heart*, relentlessly driven by forces beyond his understanding to give voice to long-silent generations who had been, for whatever reasons, unable to give their lives artistic expression, Roy believed that writing was not necessarily a voluntary occupation.

Had Roy finally realized her quest for self-knowledge? Although it would still take an incident upon her return to London to finally close the door on her theatrical ambitions, making her realize once and for all that she preferred and had always preferred writing her own ideas instead of reciting the words of others, the temporary paradise at Century Cottage at least allowed her to recognize and accept certain aspects of herself: her love for nature, her strong emotional attachment to it and the importance of its presence in her life; the need for respite and protection from the cares of the world; the importance of a window in front of her, availing her a glimpse of sky, downs, moors, prairies, or the Saint Lawrence; her passionate interest in her French heritage and her love of the French language; and her need for proximity to natural areas that allow for long walks in relative solitude. Gabrielle also began to come to terms with the subjects about which she would write. Almost in answer, so it seems, to her friend Esther's frustration about the rare correspondence between literature and life, Gabrielle sought to translate *actual human experience* into words written on a page.

And write she did. After completing a series of short articles on Canada inspired by Esther's curiosity about Roy's country, she impulsively sent three of them off to an editor in Paris before she had a chance to change her mind. The postmaster brought a response not too long afterward — a cheque and the stunning news that all three articles would be published shortly in the Parisian weekly *Je suis partout*. Although the amount, about five dollars, did not bring the financial security of her first novel a few years later, no royalty was ever as precious. Confessing in a conversation with Joan Hind-Smith that the poor quality and low artistic merit of the articles make them "not even worth mentioning," she nevertheless confirms that "the acceptance of my little 'compositions' by so important a newspaper did boost my morale considerably, as I had published almost nothing until then" (80).

Approximately two years earlier, in fact, Roy had published a murder mystery in Montreal's *Le samedi*, "La grotte de la mort" (The Cave of Death), for which she was paid very little. In fact, she lied to her derisive mother about the two dollars she had received from the Montreal paper, telling her that the amount was only an instalment. That situation recalls the reaction of Christine's mother in the story "To Earn My Living . . ." when she scoffs at the youngster's desire to support herself through writing:

> "Oh, maybe I'll earn my living by writing . . . a little later . . . before too long. . . ."
> "You poor girl!" said my mother; and after a silence, after a sigh, she continued, "Wait first until you have lived! You've plenty of time. But in the meantime, in order to live, what do you expect to do? . . ." (*Street* 238)

When she was eleven years old, the young Gabrielle had sat on her bed and jotted down two stories about her uncles for her first novel, *A Novel in Twelve Chapters* (which her mother found irreverent and consequently burned). Sitting on her comfortable bed in Century Cottage, Roy turned again to her roots for inspiration. Certainly her experiences had matured Roy and provided necessary confidence, but it is equally true to say that "Not until a mature and more independent-minded

Gabrielle had placed an ocean between herself and the constraints she'd felt at home, was she able to make a tangible commitment to live by her wits and her pen" (Manitoba Heritage Council 7).

Je suis partout published Roy's three articles about Canada, beginning in October 1938 with "Les derniers nomades" (The Last Nomads), followed by "Noëls canadiens français" (French Canadian Christmas in December) and "Comment nous sommes restés Français au Canada" (How We Remained French in Canada) in August 1939. Roy also published a few articles in 1938 on European local colour, including her own trip to Bruges, in Winnipeg's French-language newspaper, *La liberté et le patriote*, as well as an article about Lady Francis Ryder in Montreal's *Le devoir*. Roy's European sojourn continued to influence her journalism, as we shall see, upon her resettlement in Montreal, where she published a few more articles about her impressions of England, Paris, and Provence before turning to other matters, including exposés on immigrant life in Canada and the serious plight of the poor in Montreal.

In important ways, then, the weeks spent with the Perfects were nearly perfect. In the mornings, Roy wrote, propped up in that big brass bed by pillows, her typewriter on her knees. Fortified by breakfast brought to her room by Esther, her newfound guardian angel, Roy would habitually then write another four to five hours. The rest of the day was carefree, with Esther seeing to the household chores but generally free to accompany Roy on afternoon walks through fields, moors, and forest. Having vacated her flat above the bicycle shop, her only ties to London now were her weekly drama tutorials, when she met individually with Mme Gachet to recite lines from Racine or Molière. For a time, the single blight to her summer happiness took the form of letters from her mother, letters which by their mere presence dredged up all her prior sufferings, letters which inadvertently made her feel guilty for the innocent pleasures of her stay at Century Cottage, letters which, contrary to her mother's intentions, slowly cemented Gabrielle's resolve against returning to Manitoba.

Eventually, Stephen intruded into this Eden. But far from being the snake in the garden, he brought Gabrielle something she truly yearned for — shared pride in her work. Stephen praised the aspiring writer's talent, predicting as Bohdan once had that one day she would eventually make something of herself as an author. Only later did she discern that the work Stephen singled out for special praise was writing that she came to consider superficial, comic, and insubstantial. Nevertheless, sitting side by side as Stephen corrected, criticized, and lauded her work, Gabrielle experienced the satisfaction of knowing, once the animal magnetism between them ceased to dominate their time together, that she and Stephen actually did share much in common, and this harmony between two minds turned her former resentment and hurt into compassion and tenderness. Later on, when the two were alone together in the woods, the pleasant meeting of minds was once again transformed into passion, but a passion all too soon undermined by Stephen's ardent political commitments and battles. Freshly ensnared in Stephen's trap, Gabrielle's feelings that afternoon quickly cooled into certitude. And as Stephen walked away from Century Cottage, citing urgent clandestine business in London as the reason for his not spending the night, Gabrielle, somewhat relieved, mentally pictured his progress through the familiar trees and fields toward the bus that would carry him out of her life — this time, forever.

LEAVING EDEN

A harsher reality remained to be dealt with, for World War II hovered. During her "retreat," as Roy discovered on her infrequent trips to the city, London had changed in alarming ways. War preparations included digging gaping trenches in beautiful Hyde Park, plastering the city with patriotic posters meant to boost British morale, posting arrows pointing citizens to air-raid shelters, and hanging signs urging Londoners to equip themselves with gas masks. Equally disconcerting, the once crowded shops were now empty. The air of disquiet and distraction somehow drew Roy to London, and away from Century Cottage, where she had discovered a pastoral oasis that would take many forms in her life, a place of retreat so vital to her own sense of well-being, but one also that caused her to neglect people in the outside world who cared about her. A lunch with her New Zealand friend, the impeccably "Britishified" David, who now worked at the Admiralty, punctured the fragile balloon of her refuge in Epping Forest. War, David convinced her, would come, perhaps very soon.

Having collected her few things from the Perfects, Roy chose to rent a room in Chiswick, owing, perhaps, to its proximity to Kew Gardens, where she would spend the better part of many days learning exotic details about trees and flowers from all over the world. Chiswick also had the attraction of being a stop on the Green Line bus route to Epping Forest. Not unexpectedly, on her return to London she fell into the same and now familiar unsociable habits as during her first days there, reading a lot, but now writing some, and roaming around the gardens. Moved eventually by the brewing international crisis, and still subject, undoubtedly, to the aftershocks of her love affair, Roy cast herself adrift during September and October of 1938 — the period in which British prime minister Neville Chamberlain signed the infamous Munich Agreement with Adolf Hitler and returned to England declaring that the pact with the Nazis ensured "peace in our time." Bestirring herself, finally, she mustered the courage to go to one of Lady Frances's teas despite the evident possibility of Stephen's attendance. Delighted to see Roy again while at the same time urging the young woman to return quickly to Canada, Lady Frances also secured two wonderful invitations for Gabrielle to visit stately homes. Too indecisive to refuse the offer, Roy found herself at the mercy of the British gentry, but this time in the hands of those willing to befriend her and intent on making her stay in England memorable.

Despite the gracious hospitality extended during her two visits — one to Itton Court in Monmouthshire, where the principal activity was hunting, and another to an Elizabethan cottage in Dorset, where she acted more as a friend and travelling companion to her aged hostess and the woman's finicky pooch than as a guest — Roy returned to Chiswick and its rainy skies more despondent than ever. Oddly enough, the desolate landscapes of England, treeless and barren, perhaps reminding her of her beloved Manitoban prairies, had done more to lift her spirits than did social contacts and theatregoing in London. The last thing to enter Gabrielle Roy's mind after all these months in Europe, it seems, was the fact that she often felt homesick. And her attempts to avoid this difficult truth make complete sense, for although she loved Manitoba, Roy even now must have realized the huge price she must pay if she returned to Saint-Boniface and surrendered all that she had gained during the time at Epping Forest. Better to put off as long as possible the inevitable return to Canada and to the painful choices that awaited her arrival.

Still indolent and antisocial, Roy once again realized that she needed to do something with herself. She heard about an experimental theatre near Chiswick that promised its students small roles as well as the chance to attend rehearsals of other plays being staged, an opportunity reminiscent of the one with the Pitoëffs in Paris; but this time around Roy had to pay. And so she did, still torn between writing and acting as a suitable profession. Despite the moderate publishing success she had recently enjoyed, Roy continued to put off making "the irrevocable decision to be a writer," as Joan Hind-Smith explains, for fear of "taking a big step, of finding herself challenged and alone" (73). And so she continued to vacillate and, it must be said, to fool herself. Unfortunately for Gabrielle at the time but happily for her future readers, this theatre school proved less genuine than what the Pitoëffs had offered. She complained of the false promises and advertisement to Canada House in London, but the officials managed to recover only half her fees. Her funds now almost as low as her spirits, Roy longed to return, as it were, to the past, to happier environs, to Esther and Father Perfect, refusing to imagine in this time of need, even in the dead of winter, that their cottage could be anything other than warm and surrounded with flowers. Reality quickly closed this avenue of escape when Roy learned that Father Perfect, although himself in poor health, was about to embark on a trip to be with his dying sister. Roy's despair was such that she selfishly tried to dissuade Esther from such a trip, arguing disingenuously that since Father Perfect would eventually be reunited with his sister in the afterlife, he would be better off staying put — where, conveniently enough, Roy could then visit them. Undeterred, the good-hearted Esther emphasized the necessity for people, despite personal cost or inconvenience, to say good-bye to one another while on earth. This conversation had a twofold effect on Gabrielle: she found herself without a refuge, and she realized, when reminded of her own mother's silent suffering back in Manitoba, the implications of not meeting once again with those you love before they die. Throughout her life, Roy often found satisfaction and happiness in short supply when she seemed to need them the most.

As we grow older and become more self-reflective, past events, which we may have deemed insignificant at the time, in retrospect form part of a greater cause-and-effect continuum determined largely by our personal choices. Gabrielle Roy, suffering from an overdose of London fog and of disenchantment, not surprisingly fell ill. A visit to an otolaryngologist (an ear, nose, and throat specialist) proved ultimately felicitous. How lucky to have infected sinuses and badly damaged mucous membranes thanks in part to a congenitally delicate constitution and thanks also to the financial straits which had forced her mother to turn down the heat as far as possible even during the coldest of Manitoban nights. Constantly talking in a raised voice and breathing in chalk dust during her years as a teacher had most likely aggravated her condition. While these symptoms would catch up with Roy in her sixties, waking her at night on the brink of suffocation and inciting fears that she would die of asthma as did two of her brothers, back in London in early 1939 her illness translated into a most happy prognosis: she must surrender her dreams of becoming an actor, for her throat would never endure a stage career. Door closed. The end of a pursuit that was going nowhere anyway. The doctor's admonition and proscription lifted a huge weight from Roy's shoulders, for knowing that something definite though not necessarily pleasant had been determined gave her at least a certain peace. Advised by the specialist to do exactly what she had always wanted to do, she bought herself one more hiatus before confronting the daunting, frightening career as a writer that had waited for nearly thirty years. Among other things, the doctor advised a change of climate.

RECOVERY IN PROVENCE

Roy went to southern France, a locale that would always hold a special place in her heart, for three glorious months in the company of an English-speaking compatriot from Toronto she had picked up along the way. Plain, plump, and dowdy, Ruby Cronk was a nurse who proved to be a true Florence Nightingale during the difficult channel crossing, taking charge of Roy, whose nausea during the boat trip, compounded by her lingering illness, reduced her to utter misery. In her depressed and feverish condition, Roy could think only in negative terms, convinced that after Provence she would be returning to Canada at the end of her two years' quest and relative independence with nothing to show for her endeavours. The disabling depression that plagued so much of her stay in Europe, and which certainly she had hoped to leave behind in Canada, seemed in her present state destined to cloud her final months in Europe. As a result, throughout this desperate although temporary seasickness, her sense of failure and her loss of hope threatened, once again, to overwhelm her. Ruby, however, became not only Roy's nurse but also her saviour. Conveniently and graciously, Ruby took charge of Roy, her trunk, her passport, everything: she ushered her

FIGURE 3

A rare glimpse of a young, unfettered Gabrielle, circa 1943.

sick friend through customs and helped her board the train, first to Paris and afterwards to Nice, which happened to be Ruby's destination as well. During the long train rides, Ruby administered medicine to help Roy sleep and kept guard over their otherwise empty compartment so that the invalid could stretch out as she slept. Ruby went so far as to fabricate a story — largely through gestures since she knew only a handful of words in French — to ensure her patient's comfort, indicating to passengers, some of whom consequently stood for the entire trip, that a potentially contagious virus afflicted the sleeping Gabrielle. The following morning, Roy, thanks partially to the stranger-become-friend, experienced a rebirth equal in its intensity to the experience of her first days in Epping Forest. In the company of her latest guardian angel, Roy awoke, as from a bad dream, to a dazzling sky, warm air, the blue Mediterranean Sea, and picturesque villas surrounded by flowers and orange trees. Another crisis survived!

And what a jewel awaited their investigation, the Riviera of the 1930s, quiet, beautiful, and still relatively untrammelled. Within this terrestrial paradise, hope, that elusive commodity so lacking in Roy's life, returned, and with it laughter, spontaneity, and energy. What better way to thank her tired and unadventuresome friend of only twenty-four hours than to lead her on foot and by bus on a merry chase against time through one of nature's most beautiful landscapes. Roy's ability to infect others with her own enthusiasm, on those not common occasions when living simply thrilled her, worked once again. For gratefully spared from two weeks of redundant card games with old ladies in an English-speaking hotel, Ruby happily played Sancho Panza to Roy's Don Quixote, and the two young women experienced together some of the happiest times of their entire lives. (Indeed, years later, although the two had not maintained contact, Ruby confessed as much in a letter to her friend, the now-famous author. Sadly, the day Roy planned to travel to visit her now ailing friend with whom she had shared those marvellous adventures in Provence, Ruby passed away.)

While the beginning of the war became every day more inevitable, Roy and Ruby took advantage of the transitory enchantment Provence offered. Outfitted with matching clothing, decent walking shoes, and knapsacks, the two Canadians set out for adventure in a way uncommon to the times and especially uncommon for two women, in a manner that those of us who have backpacked around a Europe more heavily travelled since the 1950s can only envy. Roy experienced, probably for the first time in her life, that ideal state of carefree and unfettered youth. There in Provence, with unassuming Ruby to lean on, she temporarily shed both the memories and the oppressions of her care-stricken youth and the anxieties about her future life as an author. In the midst of this enchantment, memories intervened, to be sure, of her sorrow over Stephen or for her mother, who had struggled so much to give her children hope for the happiness that Roy truly felt during these few precious weeks. Still, living simply for the moment — a feeling duplicated only in her depiction of life in the Little Water Hen, an experience she later admitted to having idealized ("It seems to me that I tried to kill myself with work in order to kill my boredom and depression" [*Fragile* 187]) — Roy forgot the anguishes of the past, and the future was of little consequence. Roy's happiness radiated to such an extent that she made friends wherever her travels took her and inadvertently broke the hearts of many would-be Latin lovers!

Holding happiness so palpably in her hand profoundly affected this woman whose life seemed more obviously programmed for sorrow. Yet even happiness can sometimes seem a privilege reserved for the few who have the leisure to desire it. Although relatively untouched by the events in Europe preceding World War II, Roy came face to face with the human tragedy of the Spanish Civil War. When the Catalan front broke in the winter of 1939, refugees, often at the rate of twenty thousand a day, poured through the Pyrenees into a village where Roy happened one day to travel by bus, not far from her home base in Perpignan. Befriended there by some

Red Cross volunteers, she obtained a pass that allowed her free access to the spectacle of horror: the emaciated, the grotesque, the lost, the never-to-be-found, a few sick animals with festering sores slaughtered and eaten to prolong the horror a few more days, a village of two thousand trying to cope with a hundred thousand orphans, mothers with babies born in the snows of the Pyrenees, the wounded, the militants intent on returning to Spain who would probably be shot as soon as they reached the border. Roy moved about through it all, trying to help and taking photographs with her Brownie camera, until security police obliged Roy, along with others who had no reason to be there, to leave. Back in her cold room in Perpignan, Roy coped with her despair and sorrow over the human condition by the best means available to her: writing. She soon sent her reactions, along with a few photographs, to the Montreal newspaper *La presse*, but they made it no farther than some editor's wastebasket, for her story never appeared in print.

Deeply affected by her indirect experience of the Spanish Civil War, Roy returned to Paris, trying to forgive herself for her short, joy-filled holiday, which now seemed so very out of sync with the recent events she had witnessed, a foreshadowing of the terror that would soon grip nearly all of Europe. Roy never wrote directly and in vivid, horrific detail of war's terrors; she did, however, chronicle with great passion the indirect, sometimes bitterly ironic, and always destructive consequences of war for the poor inhabitants of Montreal's Saint-Henri district in her first novel, *The Tin Flute*.

As Roy returned to Paris and retraced her earlier steps from the fall of 1938, nothing seemed familiar, except perhaps Charlotte at Mme Jouve's, who still played her piano eight hours a day, oblivious to the outside world. Mme Jouve, in her own way, scolded Roy sympathetically for her continued indecision, her aimless wandering, her unnecessary restlessness. The chided French Canadian could offer no answer. Even later in life, after great success as a writer, she still could formulate no definitive response, for her later years, in

FIGURE 4

The multiple-prizewinning author in London in 1948.

significant ways, duplicated the patterns set during that time in Europe. She either fell into a waiting state with occasional moments of freedom, when she again felt almost happy but then suffered in turn from her own inactivity, or in writing suffered from the anxiety of perhaps not being equal to her past achievements. As she explained to John J. Murphy, writing is "a career . . . hampered by doubts as to the quality of one's talent" (454). And so, in a quandary that seems never to have fully left her since her arrival with that huge trunk in Paris nearly two years earlier, Roy again returned to London to visit briefly with the Perfects before sailing to Canada.

At the Perfects' cottage, all was cold, muddy, and damp, the smell of rot permeating the walls. Fortunately, later in life, Roy would visit both Mme Jouve and the Perfects under much happier circumstances. In 1947, with the Prix Femina in hand for *The Tin Flute* and a wedding band on her finger, she sought out Mme Jouve. Not surprised by her former lodger's success, Jouve confided in Roy her belief all along in her French Canadian's potential to go far as long as she did not falter on a path demanding much moral courage. Eventually wearying of the brouhaha over the Prix Femina, Roy repeated her actions of a few years earlier and fled to London, to Epping Forest in hopes of rediscovering the security, peace of mind, and love she had known at Century Cottage. Arriving this time in summer, all her former, happy memories were revived. And so was the marvellous creativity she had previously experienced while living with the Perfects.

Both Esther and her father were still alive and relatively unchanged. Her room, too, as airy as ever with its windows open to the downs, remained conducive to writing. Roy had only recently conceived the general outline for what eventually became her second book (*Where Nests the Water Hen*, which she dedicated to her husband, Dr. Marcel Carbotte). During a drive to Chartres Cathedral with her husband and friends, the northern Manitoba landscape she had experienced while teaching for five dollars a day that summer of 1937 crystallized suddenly in her mind, "a place intact, as if only just emerged from the Creator's dream" (*Fragile* 189). Inspired undoubtedly by her memories of both places of sanctuary, the Little Water Hen and Century Cottage, Roy awoke in Epping Forest one tranquil morning and suddenly, in another stunning moment of lucidity, knew who must populate her stories about the Little Water Hen — the Tousignant family: "They appeared to me — particularly Luzina — as young as the dawn of life" (*Fragile* 189). And this character, one of the author's most remarkable creations, breathes life into the narrative. Once again when she entered Roy's bedroom, Esther Perfect found her friend propped up on the bed with papers scattered over the covers. Here at Century Cottage, Roy composed the better part of her second book.

But on a sombre winter day in 1939, when she sailed from London, Gabrielle still had long years ahead of her before these happy events. France and Great Britain on the eve of World War II had nothing more to offer her. And her funds were very nearly exhausted. The time had come for her return to Canada.

THE ROAD FROM SAINT-BONIFACE

Gabrielle Roy returned to Canada, but not to her native Saint-Boniface in Manitoba. As Agnès Whitfield notes, ultimately "the young Manitoban preferred the precarious life of a freelance journalist in Montreal to the more certain and more traditional life of a teacher" (54; our translation). Did her past experience of living in a Francophone community that was tangential to, which translated often enough as inferior to, the Anglophone world of nearby Winnipeg and most of Manitoba cause her to seek refuge in the French-speaking part of her country? Such an explanation may account in part for her decision to head no farther west; it does not, however, reconcile itself easily to the transfiguration through her pen of Manitoba as something of a paradise and of Saint-Boniface as generally ordered and safe, both locales in many ways insulated from the complexities that characterize life in the world outside their boundaries. But these are the Manitoba and Saint-Boniface depicted from the safety of half a continent's distance, where distance itself perhaps allowed her the only means to reconcile herself to what she had abandoned. As Roy later wrote, repeating a quotation she attributed to André Gide, "Before discovering new shores, we must be content to lose sight of land completely" (*Fragile* 186).

But in the very real world of 1939, the loving safety Saint-Boniface offered also translated into stifling confinement. Roy's desire for independence had been a motivating factor behind the two-year stay in Europe — indeed, she had originally planned only a one-year absence — and in her mind, going farther west from Montreal would now mean a surrender to all she had sought to escape. A return to Saint-Boniface would demote those two years in Europe to the status of a fling, and it would also preclude the possibility of further personal and professional growth. Roy had turned thirty that March, and she was hardly prepared to "retire" to the past. Saint-Boniface must have struck her as offering a future of spinsterhood devoted to the care both of other people's children in her capacity as a teacher and of her ailing seventy-one-year-old mother and her mentally ill sister, Clémence. In fact, the two letters from Saint-Boniface that greeted her on arrival in Montreal seemed to portend just such a fate. They must have reinforced Gabrielle's fears and bolstered her resolve. One, from the Saint-Boniface School Board, pointed out that no extension on her two-year leave of absence would be forthcoming and requested that Roy either return to her former position at the school or promptly send her resignation. The other, from her mother, chronicled how Mélina ached for her youngest child's return, discussing how much better off each of them would be by joining her meagre funds with Roy's teaching salary and living together once again. One sentence in particular worked to confirm the daughter's worst fear. Mélina wrote, "And with you so independent and me probably too possessive, I'll try to get used to letting you lead your own life" (qtd. in *Enchantment* 406). Roy describes in her autobiography looking intently at her distorted face in the mirror and feeling the all too familiar knot in the throat that afflicted her youth, a physical reminder from the "days of greatest hardship, perpetual fears, and all that futile courage" (407).

After much pounding of the pavement, Gabrielle Roy made one of the most anguished, selfish, and painfully ambivalent decisions of her life, as decisions based largely on one's personal desires and welfare often must be. Clearly, much in Roy's life had changed over the past two years, for among other things, she had learned a good deal about herself and her ambitions. Wishing now to fulfil her own dreams, Roy could look back on her recent past and recall the psychological turmoil that would afflict her future fictional Christine in "To Earn My Living . . . ," who despite her misgivings about being a teacher as opposed to a writer, nevertheless accepts a job, as had the young Gabrielle, at a small school in Cardinal: "When as yet you scarcely know yourself, why should you not strive to realize the dream that those who love you have dreamed on your behalf?" (*Street* 240). After posting a note to the school board notifying it of her resignation, Roy penned a difficult letter to her mother, knowing that the news would hurt Mélina and anger many other concerned individuals and friends. As late as 1976, David Cobb noted that as a consequence of Roy's leaving for London and Paris and then deciding to remain in Montreal, "Some members of her family have never forgiven her" (10). Family members had considerable influence on this youngest member of the Roy household, and they could and often did wound Roy. But despite the dreadful guilt she knew would afflict her, Roy reached her decision. She softened the blow to her mother by promising to return to Saint-Boniface in a year, but she knew in her heart at this important juncture in her life that she would probably never return on a permanent basis.

More than memories of her hardships as a youth accounted for the knot that constricted Roy's throat, for Saint-Boniface also represented the loving bonds attached in particular to her mother, who had long been and would remain a dominant force in Roy's life and in her literature. As she often said, "What would I have been without the memory of my mother" (qtd. in Manitoba Heritage Council 4). However, not even the strength of love for her mother or Roy's ties to other family members could blot out the daily battles for subsistence, both physical and psychological, that characterized her formative years in Manitoba. Life there had simply been too hard, and the quest to better the family's situation seemed at times almost futile. Indeed, this pressure, this constant teetering on the edge of poverty, took its toll, in one form or another, on all Roy's family members. Inasmuch as family and place are central to all Gabrielle Roy's work, and because recollections of the past from which she actively separated herself in Montreal form the nucleus of so much of her literature, a closer look at the complex forces at play behind this knot in Roy's throat is clearly necessary. An examination of some of Gabrielle's family history may clarify her conflicted feelings, as well as reveal the creative forces and memories that inspired her writing.

EXILE FROM ACADIA

Roy's mother, Mélina Landry, was born in Quebec to Elie Landry (born at Saint-Jacques-l'Achigan, Quebec; died in Somerset, Manitoba, on 6 August 1912) and Emilie Jeansonne Landry (born in Saint-Jacques-l'Achigan in 1831; died in Saint-Boniface on 7 March 1917). Their family roots in turn hark back to Acadia (New Brunswick and Nova Scotia), a region today that begins to reclaim its rights as a geographical region and as a distinctive society with its own unique stories to tell, thanks to writers such as Antonine Maillet. Gabrielle Roy's ancestors were among those deported by the British from Acadia during the "Grand Dérangement" that took place between 1755 and 1762, scattering the French-speaking exiles throughout Canada and the United States. One group of deportees stayed together to settle in Connecticut. Subsequently, French priest-colonizers in search of flocks to settle in Quebec attracted numbers of the exiled Acadians back to Canada. Some of Roy's forebears remained in Connecticut, while others resettled in Saint-Jacques-l'Achigan, where her maternal grandparents eventually met and married. From there they moved farther north, to barren hills and to lands full of rocks, at Saint-Alphonse-de-Rodriguez. True to the pastoral tradition fostered in early Canadian fiction, in such novels as Louis Hémon's *Maria Chapdelaine* — a decidedly soft-focused portrayal of Canadian life, incidentally, that the grim reality of the Montreal working poor depicted in *The Tin Flute* would transform — Roy's maternal grandparents, thanks to strong backs and hard work, cleared the land of trees and dug up untold numbers of stones to enable them to plant their meagre crops of oats and buckwheat. Their success, while not sensational, at least allowed them to replace their original cabin with a decent house in which Mélina, Roy's mother, was born and remembered being very happy. Soon enough, along came another French priest, this time seducing his listeners with glowing accounts of the rich, fertile land of the Canadian west that awaited their arrival. He also appealed to the parishioners' patriotic duty to settle land traversed earlier by intrepid French explorers. To sweeten the West's lure, the priest further promised that the new province of Manitoba (admitted in 1870) would not only grant land to each family and to male children over the age of eighteen but would also respect their rights to both their language and their religion, two considerations for which they had previously been persecuted. And so the Landry family pulled up roots and headed West.

Interestingly enough, after the publication of *The Tin Flute*, Gabrielle Roy nursed the idea, never brought to fruition, of writing a historical novel about this westward movement. The projected narrative would offer a sort of historic tableau depicting the migration of these Québécois settlers at the end of the nineteenth century and their subsequent colonization of the prairies. As François Ricard explains in his fine study *Gabrielle Roy*, Roy did write a few hundred pages between 1945 and 1950 describing these pioneers whose relatives, like her own in Manitoba, dotted the Canadian prairies. But because the genre ill-suited her artistic inclinations and temperament, she eventually gave up on the project (112–13). Roy refused to give up, however, on the notion of depicting in her fiction and in her nonfiction the at times painful and hardly idyllic reality these weary immigrant travellers often confronted on the harsh plains of Manitoba and provinces farther west. The line "But plants are like people" (Enchanted Summer 19), for example, characterizes neither the relative simplicity nor the wondrous adventure of people's transporting themselves to unfamiliar lands, motifs common to much of earlier Canadian literature; instead, the figurative language underscores the fact that like plants, transplanted people face daunting challenges, including, among other things, hostile or infertile environments that leave them without new roots. As Allison Mitcham emphasizes, the quotation "leads to the insight so basic to Roy's work that rootless people are essentially as vulnerable as rootless plants — and indeed the majority of her most touching characters are rootless" ("Roy's West" 162). These mostly hopeful people searching to transplant themselves include the displaced French-speaking immigrants from Quebec described by Roy in The Road Past Altamont, who, like her ancestors, struggle to eke out a life for themselves in Manitoba. Often they resemble the pathetic and impoverished French family moving from the prairie to the city in "The Move," a family the youthful narrator describes as "people who were doomed to a life of which I knew nothing, terribly gray and, it seemed to me, without exit" (Road 99).

Drawn by the promise of fertile land, Roy's ancestors settled in Saint-Léon on the slope of the Pembina Escarpment in south-central Manitoba, the grandfather hoping to console his wife for the loss of her much-loved Laurentian Highlands with the small hills that particular region offered. But these impostors for hills, as Roy writes in her essay "My Manitoba Heritage," only aggravated the poor woman's homesickness: "the sight of these pretentious little humps was to sharpen her regret at ever having left the steep slopes of her youth" (*Fragile* 143). The sight of the hills likewise fostered within the family a love forever divided between plains and mountains, but as Roy writes, "it is in their divided loves that artists and others find their hurts and treasures," a conflict, to be sure, central to Roy's work, for even sorrow is not without enchantment (*Fragile* 144). Starting over again, Elie Landry and thousands of others like him built houses identical to those left behind in Saint-Alphonse and the other towns from which they had journeyed, thus creating small Québécois villages all over southern Manitoba. Elie Landry and his sons owned a fairly prosperous square mile of land — prosperous, that is, until Manitoba passed a law in 1890 that abolished public funding for Catholic schools and forbade the use of the French language for instruction in the schools. To support alternative French-language schools for their children, Franco-Manitobans began taxing themselves and, by one of those painful ironies history often repeats, as Roy notes in her autobiography, thereby assured their own poverty.

Gabrielle knew of her father Léon's parents, the frowning Charles and his sad-looking wife, Marcelline, only from two photographs hanging on the living room wall, for her father spoke seldom of them. And based almost solely on the impressions these two pictures conjured up in her mind, Roy felt such antipathy toward these grandparents that she preferred imagining herself as entirely descended from the fun-loving, romantic, genteel Landrys. In her musings while sitting by her father's coffin — he died of pulmonary oedema in 1927 — and looking at the photographs of his parents, she felt drawn to them for the first time, seeing through their stern countenances to something more and utilizing the shreds of anecdotal information that she knew about them to bring them to life. Grandmother Roy's tight-lipped severity seemed that day to hide unspoken sorrows due as much as anything to life with a narrow-minded, uncompromising husband, "a self-appointed judge of morality" (*Enchantment* 75). A man opposed to joy, education, and even literature, he once grabbed his son's only book out of his hands and threw it into the stove fire. About the bitterness harboured in such a man Roy could only speculate. The smouldering anger of the Ukrainian postman Nick Sluzick, in *Where Nests the Water Hen*, perhaps recalls Léon Roy's father; Nick keeps his wife and daughters isolated from all humanity in the northern reaches of Manitoba and rules his family with an iron hand — no fun and certainly no dancing for *his* wife and daughters. While the loving Father Joseph-Marie — who switches from language to language for his multilingual congregation and, in one particular section, to Ukrainian for Nick's ears — sermonizes about the wonderful variety of birds in this world who must fly free, and about the need to uncage people, particularly women, Nick angrily contemplates his boots, thinking to himself that God attends to his business and Nick Sluzick takes care of his own affairs.

Not surprisingly, Léon Roy, who was born in 1850, fled his embittered, poverty-stricken home in Beaumont at a young age and struck out on his own to Quebec City, where he found employment as a salesperson in a small shop. A priest, who in retrospect truly exemplifies the Christian principles of compassion and charity, virtues also manifested in the Capuchin monk from Toutes-Aides, must have recognized in Léon a man with something to offer, for he paid for two years of university study for the young idealist. Afterward, Léon travelled around the United States, working at everything, while continuing to study and read, before ending up finally in Manitoba. In Saint-Léon he met Mélina Landry, and the two married in 1886. The young family moved to Saint-Alphonse, to Mariapolis, to Somerset, and finally settled permanently in Saint-Boniface in 1897.

Following his return to Canada, Roy's father had tied his aspirations, for better or for worse, to the Liberal politician and future prime minister of Canada (1896–1911) Wilfrid Laurier, the first French Canadian to hold that office. In addition to his full-time work as a colonizing officer (1897–1913) who founded settlements for immigrants throughout the western plains, a job he truly loved, Léon Roy was an active party organizer for Laurier's federal Liberals. Believing completely in Laurier's vision for Canada, Gabrielle's father worked enthusiastically for his election and remained an ardent supporter even when Laurier, in the opinion of many French speakers in Manitoba, traitorously refused to take sides in Manitoba French issues such as the infamous language laws that forbade French instruction in schools; Laurier preferred to leave such matters in the hands of the province itself. The wake of passion, anger, and bloodletting that followed Laurier's defeat by Robert Borden's Conservative party in the 1911 federal election saw many of those loyal to Laurier fall as well:

> Laurier's defeat was partly brought about by his own people of French descent in Quebec, who interpreted his middle-of-the-road attitude towards British imperialism versus Canadian independence as too strongly pro-British. Even the immigration policy which provided Léon with his work was suspect, since it was administered by Clifford Sifton, who was remembered for his anti-French sentiments in Manitoba. (Hind-Smith 67)

Indeed, in 1913, when Gabrielle was only four years old, Léon's loyalty cost him his beloved job, in part for refusing to change his party affiliation, as many of Laurier's fair-weather supporters did, to become a member of the victorious Conservative party. Loyal perhaps to a fault — a full-length portrait of Wilfrid Laurier adorned a wall in Léon's study at the home on Deschambault Street — the generally soft-spoken Léon would become furious with those who attacked the former prime minister. Consequently, with only six months until his retirement, Roy's father was fired from the job he had performed admirably for many years, and despite repeated pleas to government officials from those whom he had helped over the years, he found himself unemployed at the age of sixty-four, with no pension to support his family.

Léon himself suffered the humiliation of personally pleading his case, but nothing changed. In the story "By Day and by Night" from *Street of Riches*, Roy relates how Christine's aged father, who had the same job as Léon, returned from inspecting his settlements only to find a letter from the government informing him that a younger man with more modern ideas would soon replace him. And while the real-life circumstances certainly differ from the fictional account, the bitter lesson remains the same: Roy's father lost his job for refusing to change his personal and political convictions when the federal and provincial governments wanted not an experienced man, a "servant of the country, but a servant of our own" (*Street* 228). The betrayal destroyed Léon. As Roy recounted to David Cobb, her father "was an idealist, he believed only the best of people . . . and it broke him" (10). The unjust dismissal also threw the family into near poverty.

Roy's refusal pretty much throughout her life to become passionately embroiled in political affairs, a stance that resulted in sometimes harsh attacks and slurs by Quebec separatists that hurt her deeply, finds a potential source in her father's unjust dismissal. Among others who misjudged her, the critic Gaetan Dostie wrote that Roy "sees Quebec with the mystery and distance of a stranger" (qtd. in Scott), and Pierre Vallières, author of *White Niggers of America*, criticized her for not joining the vanguard of intellectuals calling for Quebec's independence from Canada (see Cobb 13). For years Roy, a federalist who lukewarmly supported some form of autonomy for Quebec, struggled to maintain both her love for Quebec and her equally powerful connection with her Manitoba heritage, that Canadian mosaic her work recounts. Obviously, many in Quebec who appreciated the social realism and criticism of government policy in *The Tin Flute* were disappointed that Roy did not become actively engaged in or sufficiently artistically motivated to write about the social, religious, and political upheaval caused by the Quiet Revolution in the French-speaking province. In response to repeated questions about this emotional issue, Roy replied that she knew of these concerns:

> So much came out in my first book, and to some extent in *The Cashier*. But I cannot force myself to write anything unless it corresponds 100 per cent with my conscience. I'm inclined to agree with the ultimate separatist aim of more autonomy — but I have a great fondness for the rest of Canada, too. To some Quebeckers that makes me a bizarre creature, my western heritage is a curse as well as, to me, a blessing. You see, I think of myself as living in a large rural house in one room. I love the whole house but it's that one room I'm completely at ease in. And that room is Quebec. (qtd. in Cobb 13)

And while she felt that many in Quebec ignored and resented her, Roy maintained these strong convictions and lived what struck many as a life of contradictions. She believed that Francophones outside Quebec could not maintain their heritage without the dominantly French-speaking province's support. In her estimation, however, Quebec had for too long ignored her brethren in the remainder of Canada, paying more attention to French groups in Louisiana, the Caribbean, or northern Africa. Like the strongest of her characters, Roy never gave up hope, dreaming of a united Canada that nurtured the country's rich diversity.

FATHER AND DAUGHTER

Gabrielle Roy, the last of Mélina and Léon's eleven children, made her debut into this family on 22 March 1909, when her mother was forty-two and her father fifty-nine. She entered the world while her pioneer father was in his heyday, healthy and indefatigable in his devotion to the job of leading "his" immigrants to the West and settling them in the virgin lands of Saskatchewan and Alberta. Very much the trailblazer depicted in American movies who guides the inexperienced newcomers through uncharted regions, sometimes he would be gone for weeks at a time, helping found villages for the newly arrived Hutterites (ardent communal pacifists of German origin), Mennonites (neither completely German nor completely Russian, arriving in Canada from the Netherlands), Doukhobors (incorrigible, mystic, indomitable Russian Christians), and Ukrainians (who called themselves the "Irish" of Canada). Roy wrote about these groups in her fiction and in many of her journalism articles, some of which are collected in *The Fragile Lights of Earth*. In a story inspired by her father and his profession, "The Well of Dunrea," Roy depicts the father of Christine, the narrator of *Street of Riches*, as an intrepid leader, a pioneer who helped "his Little Ruthenians" (*Street* 116), who called him "Mr. Government" — "If you please, Mr. Government, do us the great honor of coming to our table" (*Street* 118) — settle the Canadian prairies:

> these people believed him endowed with an almost supernatural power. Who can ever know what peace of mind, what certitude Papa felt among his Little Ruthenians? Isolated, far from any other village, not yet even speaking their neighbors' language, they must have relied wholly upon Papa, and the trust between them was total. (116–17)

Léon Roy devoted himself equally to the resettlement of French Canadians in the West to keep a fair balance between the English and the French presence there. And although many criticized the Laurier government, which put considerable emphasis on immigration to and settlement of the West, for not ensuring a more dominant French population, Léon believed fervently, as would his youngest daughter, in a united Canada. Gabrielle Roy was born when her father had just established "one of his most impressive settlements, Dollard in Saskatchewan, composed almost entirely of compatriots from the county of Dorchester in Quebec, where he was born, and the rest repatriated from the United States" (*Enchantment*

FIGURE 5

Léon Roy, Gabrielle's father, at about age seventy, circa 1920–21.

28). He often mused about how different Canada would have been had all the French-speaking exiles, Acadians and others, moved west. Before Gabrielle came to know him, her father must have had something of the legendary about him, following as he did in the footsteps of such explorers as La Vérendrye, a voyageur of the eighteenth century, committed also to the colonization and Christianization of the West, leaving in his wake here and there in Manitoba French names as testimony to his presence. He could also see himself as continuing the work of the Abbot Provencher, a Québécois missionary who established on the opposite banks of the Red River from Winnipeg the first French-Catholic mission, later to be known as Saint-Boniface.

By the time Gabrielle was old enough to take stock of the environment around her, however, the courageous, noble, blue-eyed idealist who had been her father no longer existed. In his place stood the defeated, stooped, careworn man whose air of tragedy often frightened his youngest daughter. One might think that the great diversity in their ages would have brought them together to enjoy the charming camaraderie Roy describes between the elderly Monsieur Saint-Hilaire and the young girl in "The Old Man and the Child" (*The Road Past Altamont*) who travel together to Lake Winnipeg. Roy's father, however, kept to himself, finding being a father again at his advanced age very difficult; and Gabrielle, at a young age not knowing better and at an older age too wrapped up in her own work, followed suit. Paternal as he was toward his immigrants, an attitude derived probably from his own anguished memories of childhood, Léon never learned to reach out to the "last little one," the child of his old age, whose late arrival seems to have embarrassed him at times (*Fragile* 149). One recalls the tormented elderly father in "By Day and by Night" who confesses to his very young daughter: "One shouldn't have children when one is old. . . . One can quit this world without knowing them, without knowing much about them, and that's a heartbreaking loss . . ." (*Street* 232). The converse is also sadly true, for Roy did not really come to appreciate the man her father had been until years after his death. But as she writes in "My Manitoba Heritage," her father's stories, humorous and tragic, remained dear and important to her for the remainder of her life, especially as the stories' significance relates to her vision of a unified Canada:

> My father's stories, the little trips we took with my mother, the Manitoba backdrop where the faces of all the people of the world were to be seen, all this brought the "foreigner" so close to me that he ceased to be foreign. Even today, if I hear a person living only a few miles away described as a "stranger," I cannot help feeling an inner tremor as if I myself had been the victim of an insult to humanity.
>
> Either there are no more foreigners in the world, or we are foreigners all. (*Fragile* 153)

At his death, in defining her own craving for his affection coupled with an acute fear of rejection, Gabrielle realized that she and her father were, at least in the abstract, two of a kind. Among other things, both daughter and father shared a reverence for the truth. She also inherited from him an abiding interest in gardening and a love of birds; indeed, birdwatching, as reflected, for instance, in the catalogue of various birds that visit in *Enchanted Summer*, brought her great joy and relaxation. Roy was also fond of telling the story of how robins would perch on her father's outstretched arms, a feat she never saw repeated. At this moment of grief, however, she recalled only one happy memory with which to console herself — one crazy, wonderful afternoon when her old father, plucking her up and depositing her in the wheelbarrow, pushed her and their fat grey cat slowly around the house. While their relationship often seemed awkward or strained, both possessed great affection for the other; any notions that she resented him or that he disliked her are simply unsupported.

FIGURE 6

The Roy family home at 375, rue Deschambault, Saint-Boniface, Manitoba, circa 1912, where Gabrielle grew up.

Because her retired and retiring father remained for the most part out of reach, Gabrielle turned naturally to her mother, Mélina Landry Roy. That she was the youngest of eleven children, three of whom died, must also have played a role in strengthening Gabrielle's closeness to her mother since eight years separated her from the next sibling. Mélina Roy, like her husband, was of pioneer stock, having travelled as a child in a covered wagon from Quebec to Manitoba. A woman of incredible energy and resourcefulness, she was also dedicated to her youngest child. Mélina was Gabrielle's greatest proponent but, ironically, her greatest obstacle to overcome in her quest for self-identity as an author.

The opening chapter of Roy's autobiography describes her and her mother's trip to Eaton's, an Anglophone department store across the river in Winnipeg. This otherwise simple trip epitomizes many of the anguishes that haunted her youth, when she was frequently made to feel an outsider. She and her mother shopped in the bargain basement, and then only on those infrequent occasions when special sales coincided with a little extra household cash. How Mélina managed ever to have even the sparest of spare cash is perhaps a story only she could tell. Their three-storey house at 375, rue Deschambault, immortalized in *Street of Riches*, ate up its fair share of expenses, owing to high heating costs and local taxation.

Living only on ever-dwindling savings, sewing projects solicited by Mélina from family and friends, earnings from the occasional sales of acreage acquired by Léon during his travels, the rent paid by boarders and lodgers taken into their home, and occasional help from older children who had left the household such as Rodolphe and Adèle, Mélina managed to keep her family afloat. So off she and her youngest daughter would go to Eaton's, their list of purchases incommensurate with their ability to pay, but nevertheless dreaming, full of hope, their thoughts carefree. While such trips to the other side of the river gave vent to Mélina's spirit of adventure, like

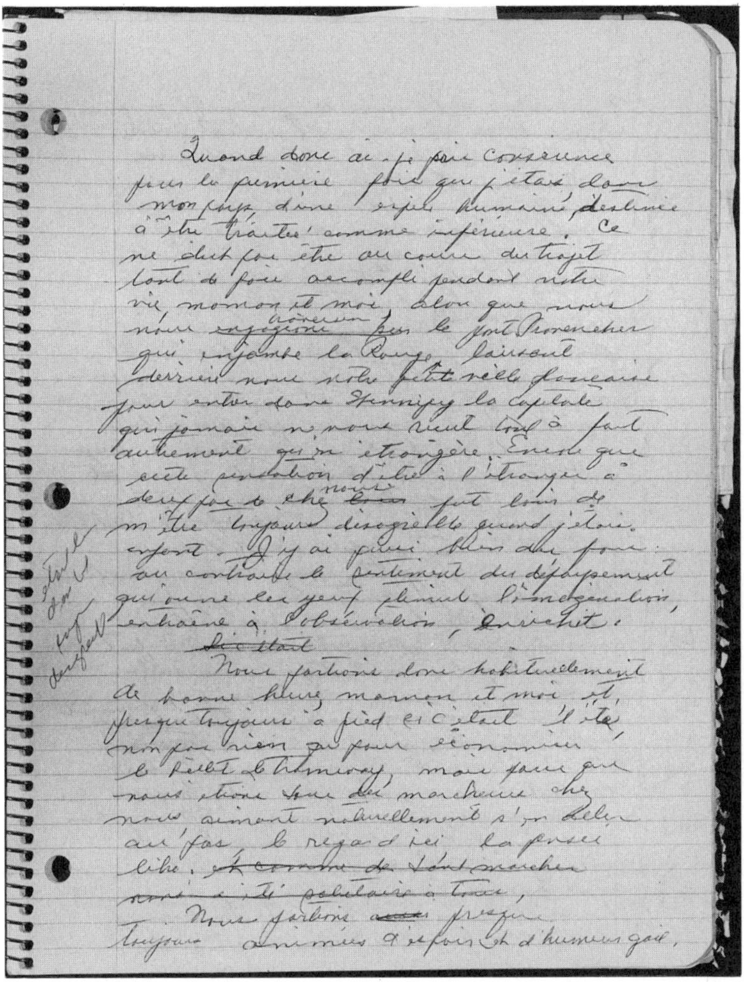

FIGURE 7

The first manuscript page of Gabrielle Roy's autobiography,
Enchantment and Sorrow (La détresse et l'enchantement),
telling of her trip with her mother to Eaton's department
store across the river in Winnipeg.

all adventures, the outcome proved risky. Once across the river, they had to ford dismal, drunken, derelict neighbourhoods before arriving at the broad and far more cheerful main streets of Winnipeg, a scenario that would repeat itself years later in the Saint-Henri district of Montreal, when a mature Roy, who could now identify with the occupants' plight, walked among the poor French Canadian neighbourhoods. In downtown Winnipeg, Gabrielle and her mother had to overcome their sense of themselves as foreigners; when chatting amiably with each other, they drew stares from the English speakers, and when they arrived at their destination, language still proved a barrier. Were Mélina feeling forceful, she would demand a French-speaking saleswoman who, more often than not, turned out to be a neighbour. On other days, defeated from the outset, Mélina would deal with a unilingual English-speaking saleswoman, the latter often calling additional personnel to help in deciphering the needs of these "foreigners" — a word Gabrielle despised, as her comments in "My Manitoba Heritage" suggest. Obliging shoppers often intervened, but although they meant to help, such a gathering of good intentions proved torture for mother and daughter; both of them often slipped away in the middle of these unpleasant negotiations while the participants continued to discuss the matter at hand. Safely on their own, their discomfiture would give way to gales of laughter, imagining as they did the crowd still debating how best to help people no longer there. One time, Mélina found herself so distraught in the midst of so much attention that she escaped down the aisles, her umbrella open as if to protect her further or to open a wider pathway. On that occasion, Gabrielle, more than a little embarrassed, berated her mother for such behaviour. Instead of feeling ashamed, however, Mélina countered with a description of her own limited education, laying the blame on Gabrielle and making her daughter feel guilty for not yet learning English, gifted and talented girl that she was. While such incidents may have helped define for Gabrielle the second-class position Francophones occupied in Manitoban society, on a more positive note these shared experiences allowed the young girl to inherit the gift of laughter from her mother. Equally as important, Gabrielle became sensitive to her mother's situation and sympathized with Mélina's daily suffering, a suffering assuaged by her hopes that her children would realize in their own lives what she could only dream of for herself. For years, the obedient, thankful, and obliging daughter worked to fulfil her mother's unfulfilled dreams.

Mélina did what she could despite the grinding, incessant reality of too little money, a poverty Gabrielle often described as "genteel," owing to all that they possessed despite economic hardship. If Gabrielle longed for a certain article of clothing, her ever-attentive mother would have her try it on at the store and then duplicate its cut, using fabric bought on sale and her own talent and ingenuity at a sewing machine (which always threatened to break down before Mélina finished paying off the monthly instalments). She also somehow found money for piano lessons for all her daughters, a necessary element, in her estimation, in the upbringing of proper young ladies.

Owing to the family's hard-pressed economic situation, Gabrielle heard her mother's question "How much?" repeated with regularity, though nothing quite prepared her for the same question when she needed, at the age of twelve, an emergency appendectomy. Ironically, years later as Gabrielle plotted her escape from Saint-Boniface, she would ask a doctor the same question when her mother needed surgery. The cost of her daughter's surgery triggered her mother's dramatic reiteration of the sad narrative of Léon's dismissal and the heartbreaking loss of his pension, along with more intimate and therefore more painful descriptions of the sewing and alterations she herself would often work at laboriously well into the night to provide her family with basic necessities. After listening to this woman's woeful tale, the doctor, who initially demanded the full payment of $100 to $150, relented and allowed Mélina to make instalments. When Mélina broke her hip about a year before Gabrielle's departure for Europe, it was Gabrielle's turn to experience the panic of having her hopes potentially dashed by financial concerns. Although the surgeon reduced his fee from $250 to $100, the sum represented such a huge dent in Gabrielle's savings, scraped together secretly and so slowly over eight years, that she, in turn, poured out her own confused story, not from the past but concerning her future, her driving need, despite a lack of definite objectives, to leave Saint-Boniface for Europe. The doctor reacted, first, by urging her, in no uncertain terms, to depart, to take hold of life before it swallowed her. Second, he not only promised to cure her mother but also left the amount of the bill and the due date to Gabrielle's conscience.

Roy admired her mother for her stoicism; she never heard her complain of physical pain, although later in life especially Mélina had good reason to do so. In addition, Roy admired her commitment to her children, for Mélina impressed her as a woman who, not unlike Rose-Anna, the perpetually house-hunting mother in *The Tin Flute*, would probably beg for alms in public if such drastic measures were required to ensure their welfare. Of her mother's relief over the affordability of her daughter's appendectomy once the doctor separated its cost into manageable instalments, Gabrielle wrote: "She was like a fine, full-flowing river whose bed is strewn from beginning to end with obstacles — boulders, rocks, and reefs — amid which she'd keep flowing, around them, over them, or wishful-thinking them away" (*Enchantment* 11). Unable to voice or define her admiration as a young adolescent, Roy responded to her mother in the best way she knew. Calling back her departing mother to her bedside after the successful operation and looking earnestly at Mélina, who seemed strangely old at that particular moment, Roy promised to come in first in her class. And seeing the distress in her mother's face give way to pride, Gabrielle knew then that she must work especially hard to keep this important promise. Just as Luzina does in *Where Nests the Water Hen*, Mélina saw education as the essential ticket for success. Obviously, given the fact that schools appear in nearly all her works, Roy felt strongly about education; she liked to say that to educate oneself and to love are almost the same thing.

A SERIOUS STUDENT

Fortunately, Roy found school easy and enjoyed learning; she must also have possessed something of a photographic memory. The incredible store of encounters, visits, travels, and family and friends from which she drew for her fiction testifies to such an ability, as does her academic success. Word for word and with an ease that never ceased to impress her teachers, she could recall in its entirety a paragraph she had just breezed through. Roy did not, however, fulfil the promise to her mother that first year after surgery, needing time to figure out just how to apply herself. After a series of illnesses that included jaundice left her too weak to attend school for another year, and with her mother's relentless self-sacrifice in attempting to keep house and household together becoming ever more apparent to the maturing youngster, Roy discovered the impetus she needed and focused her energies.

At fourteen, Gabrielle thus began to take her studies seriously. At fifteen, she resembled "an old woman," devoting extra hours to study and apparently having little time for friendships (*Enchantment* 51). Slow physiological development, moreover, probably saved her from the normal distractions of boys during this period, although attending an all-girls school probably also helped her concentration. At the conclusion of her first year of serious application, during which she forced herself awake one or two hours earlier than the rest of the household to ensure an empty kitchen in which to study, Roy fulfilled her promise to Mélina, coming in first in her class at the Académie Saint-Joseph for the first time. Her mother's radiant pride rivalled the expression on her face when Gabrielle originally made her hospital-bed promise. Roy's own pleasure in such an achievement, coupled with her strong sense of having lifted a weight from her mother's tired shoulders, only pushed her to excel even more in a domain where success made the hard work enjoyable. Year after year until she graduated, the Manitoba French Canadian Association awarded her a medal for highest marks in French. To add to her drawer full of medals accumulated during her school years, she once won the highly coveted Quebec Department of Education medal, awarded for scholastic excellence to the student with the highest marks in French in all of Manitoba.

Going to school through grade twelve in the late 1920s was an extravagant expense, and to educate women to that level was considered even more so, especially for people of limited means such as Roy's parents. To save money, her father wished his youngest to attend normal school directly after she completed eleventh grade to prepare herself to become the teacher her mother always dreamed of her becoming. Funds at rue Deschambault were running low, as always, and the last of their properties in Saskatchewan — always more a moral than financial hedge against poverty, since owning property assuaged the stigma attached to not having money — had already been sold, the money going to Adèle to repay loans she had made her parents. But the ever-persuasive Mélina, arguing for her youngest daughter's future welfare as well as her own, disagreed with her husband, pointing out that Gabrielle's not completing grade twelve would impinge on the quality of diploma their daughter would receive and subsequently lessen her chances of teaching at a city school near her parents. So Roy completed grade twelve, and all for the better. The prizes handed out by the Manitoba French Canadian Association to students in grades eleven and twelve were cash awards of fifty and of one hundred dollars respectively, and Gabrielle won both of them, using the cash to offset tuition and the cost of supplies at normal school. And before Roy's graduation in 1927, the principal of the Académie Saint-Joseph thought to check Roy's marks on the year-end Department of Education examinations, only to discover that this exemplary student had also come first in *English* for five years running.

Roy's success in French probably outweighs her parallel success in English, for in 1916 Manitoban law restricted instruction in French to only one hour a day. Roy certainly owed a debt to the dedication and fervour of the nuns and of some lay teachers who, in addition to breaking the law during school hours (as Roy herself did as a teacher), also tutored students after school hours in French for free. Apparently, inspectors from the Department of Education often closed their eyes to such passive resistance, so long as the students made requisite progress in English. Such looking the other way, however, did not preclude a tacit sense of menace, and perhaps this potential for punishment did more good than harm in sparking student achievement and interest in French by making the fruit, as it were, something forbidden.

Given the reality of the language laws, however, Roy and her classmates took the majority of their subjects in English: chemistry, physics, mathematics, Canadian history, and, obviously, English literature. In French they studied Quebec history, religion, and French literature, although the reading list was painfully uninspiring: Veuillot and Montalembert, as obscure then as they are now, and, bound to stir the young heart to nothing but sleep, the poetry of François Coppée, Sully Prudhomme, and Lamartine. Without access to Ronsard, Diderot, Corneille, Flaubert, Baudelaire, and Proust, how were the nuns to elicit any passion amongst their adolescent charges for French literature? English literature, on the other hand, came alive in these young minds through Hardy, Eliot, the Brontë sisters, and Austen, as well as poets such as Keats, Shelley, Byron, and Wordsworth. Roy was riveted.

Her first encounter with Shakespeare, a performance of *The Merchant of Venice* by a London troupe at the Walker Theatre in Winnipeg, left a lasting impression. She began to read and reread his work, at an early age laying the foundation for a lifelong love of the Bard, who always held something of the ineffable for Roy. During one of those rare and wondrous moments in life when we take centre stage and perform brilliantly, Roy once saved her class during the school inspector's visit. Unwittingly, by expressing her passion for the Bard, she soothed the inspector's amour propre by confirming to this Anglophone the superiority of his civilization. As the story goes, Roy had memorized, though without fully understanding their meaning, the famous lines from *Macbeth* that begin, "Is this a dagger which I see before me." A bit of a show-off during those years, Roy happily gave repeat performances, at the savvy nuns' request, of the moving soliloquy to impress important classroom visitors. She particularly dazzled the aforementioned inspector by rattling off the names by which the witches greet Macbeth and then launching into her increasingly polished rendition of "Is this a dagger," her accent notwithstanding. The already impressed inspector must have soared beyond ecstasy when the young thespian next offered an impassioned recitation of Coleridge's *Rime of the Ancient Mariner*. When Roy later tried to solicit praise from her austere teacher, the nun, all too wary of that deadliest of sins, pride, softened only to scoff gently but with uncanny clairvoyance, "Get out of my sight, you little romancer!" (*Enchantment* 57). Gabrielle learned her lesson, for she never forgot the admonition.

Nor did she forget what always seemed to her the rather silly and destructive extremism of the language laws of her youth which emphasized English. Later, the Quebec laws that championed French struck her as equally extreme. Indeed, in *Where Nests the Water Hen*, Roy satirizes both extremes, represented by Mademoiselle Côté, who attempts to instil Quebec nationalism in Luzina's children, and by the Victorian Miss O'Rorke, who raises the British flag over the little island and pontificates on the benefits the British Empire offers. In *Children of My Heart*, moreover, although the narratives involve a French-speaking teacher's experiences in Manitoba, presumably teaching in English, Roy makes no mention of the language question. When Gail Scott asked her about the omission in the book, Roy replied, "I wanted to keep it above that," adding that as a teacher in Manitoba she taught her Franco-Manitoban students far more French than the law allowed. As Paula Lewis writes in "The Last of the Great Storytellers," "Mme Roy believes that those authors who are

FIGURE 8

*Roy on cross-country skis. She considered
herself one of the pioneers of this sport.*

so intensely involved in politics are allowing their political concerns to supersede their literary calling" (208). Roy's childhood experiences laid a strong foundation to support her later convictions.

Roy filled her teen years with anxious study, anxious because she felt that excelling in school provided the only avenue of support she could give her mother, whose physical deterioration was becoming evident. When Roy celebrated her eighteenth birthday, her mother was sixty, and an aged sixty at that, having given birth to eleven children and having raised the eight who survived through years of hardship. Since Gabrielle participated in few social occasions during her years at secondary school, she had little to do except study. Even in her twenties, Roy kept to herself, skating a little, walking a lot. When finances permitted a bit of self-indulgence, she bought a tennis racket, a light bicycle which was her "pride and joy," and even a too long pair of second- or thirdhand skis which transformed her into a "pioneer of cross-country skiing," blazing trails across the prairie landscape (*Enchantment* 51).

During these years, Roy was obviously learning many things about herself. She discovered not only that academic studies came easily to her but also that she happened to be very competitive; coming first in her class gave her considerable satisfaction, and she therefore took it very badly one year when she finished second. Such a driving need to win may account in part for the importance solitude assumed in her life after the success of her first novel, *The Tin Flute*. Bad reviews or low book sales took enough of a toll that her most effective weapon against the resulting anguish became to ignore both. Her fanaticism about whatever task she undertook was only aggravated by her perfectionism. To protect her teenage daughter from her overstudious self, at times Mélina felt compelled to take out a fuse, cutting the current to Roy's bedroom and forcing her to go to bed at a reasonable hour. Her exceptional drive as a student, an important quality for success, portended much about Roy's future life as a writer. For example, when she completed *The Tin Flute*, Roy became

FIGURE 9

*Roy's graduating class at the Académie Saint-Joseph in 1927.
Gabrielle is seated in the centre of the front row.*

FIGURE 10

*Roy's graduation photograph, 1927. The white dress, roses,
and photograph meant even more self-sacrifice by her mother.*

very ill, so exhausted that she feared she might die. She consulted a doctor, telling him that she was a writer and did not actually work. As she relates the anecdote to Donald Cameron, the doctor told her that her work was killing her, but Roy adds, "he had a long time persuading me that I was exhausted through eight or ten hours of writing per day" (140). She maintained a similar schedule throughout her professional career, and it comes as no surprise that much later in life her doctors ordered her to "retire" from writing after she had suffered a heart attack and was in failing health.

By the time of her graduation from grade twelve, the medals and awards she had acquired — ho-hum, another one to add to the drawer reserved for such honours — meant little to her, as is often the case when victories come too easily. The principal of the Académie Saint-Joseph, to celebrate Roy's impressive academic successes and the unusually large group of graduates, decided to make the graduation a grand affair: the twelve young women would wear white dresses and white shoes, and pose together for a two-dollar photograph, holding their identical bouquets of red roses (Gabrielle's first, purchased at the exorbitant cost of five dollars) in their left arms near their hearts. This crowning glory of Roy's achievement, however, meant extra hardship for her mother. The daughter's insouciance at this point in her life, no more and no less than that of most young adults, is forgivable. Despite the financial stress such a graduation caused the Roy family, few dresses have been stitched with more pride and self-sacrifice than the dress Mélina Roy laboured over for her daughter's happiness. And Mélina's selflessness on behalf of Gabrielle was never more apparent than at that graduation. In the middle of the ceremony, Gabrielle looked down from the stage, searching out her mother's face. What she saw remained forever with her: "Her poor face was grey with fatigue . . . [and] suddenly I knew how much all this had cost" (Enchantment 60). Roy's revelation — the fact that sorrow and joy are not mutually exclusive, that the presence of one never abolishes the other, that they often occur simultaneously: anguish in the midst of joy, and the heart ever grateful for the joy felt even in an ocean of sorrow — reappears in various guises throughout her works. The ideal, she often repeated, is to elicit laughter and tears simultaneously (see, for example, Delson-Karan 196). And so in her autobiography, appropriately entitled *Enchantment and Sorrow* (*La détresse et l'enchantement*), Roy recalls that crucial moment in her development when she discerned her mother's face in the crowd and experienced fully the contradiction that comes to function as a major theme throughout her oeuvre.

ENCHANTED SUMMERS

Despite all the *détresse* growing up poor and French-speaking in Manitoba caused, Roy often experienced *enchantement*, particularly during the summers spent at Uncle Excide's, the younger of the Landry sons. As it did Mélina, life endowed Excide with a flair for laughter even in times of misfortune. Gabrielle's deep fascination and love for the prairies grew out of these trips to her uncle's. Excide's farm was located about two miles from Somerset, a small city southwest of Winnipeg and about thirty miles north of the border with North Dakota. The high point of the train trip to Somerset occurred when the landscape changed about an hour out of Winnipeg where flatlands gave way almost imperceptibly to hills, those impostor mountains that did not impress Roy's grandmother. The train stopped for a few minutes at Babcock, a name used later in *Children of My Heart* for the hills into which the narrator and one of her male students ride. Babcock's notoriety, at least for the young Gabrielle, lay in the view the location afforded of Pembina Mountain, in actuality no more than a slight elevation with rocky flanks. The anticipation of its sight nevertheless dominated Gabrielle's and her mother's conversation until the train reached Babcock; afterwards, the memory of its sight eclipsed all others for the remainder of the trip. The magic of youth. In later years, neither the Rockies nor the Alps stirred Roy more. When she intentionally revisited this area

as an adult, however, she had difficulty distinguishing anything more than some stones and a sort of natural butte.
Adulthood often quashes the magic in our lives, but that magic
can sometimes be restored to us in small doses by writers such
as Gabrielle Roy who possess the gift of recapturing lost
dreams and half-remembered visions from our youth.

After Babcock, the train traversed a different kind of prairie,
this area rolling and waving in the wind, stretching under
Manitoba's sky toward a seemingly never-ending horizon.
Once, on arriving at the Somerset station, Roy heard the
handbell at a nearby hotel ringing for lunch, a detail she used
years later in *Enchanted Summer*.

Escorted by her Uncle Excide in his Ford back to the farm,
Gabrielle, her mother, and other family members actually
travelled back in time to the family origins in Quebec. The
heart of the Landry family began in Saint-Léon, a town southeast of Somerset, six or seven miles beyond Excide's farm.
Grandfather Landry had obtained his concession at Saint-
Léon from the Manitoban government and, along with his
sons, brought a square mile of rich earth under cultivation.
There, too, he built his home, replicating the one left behind
at Saint-Alphonse-de-Rodriguez, Quebec. The neighbours,
also pioneers from Quebec, had names like Rondeau, Géné-
reux, Lussier, and Labossière. Within this community the
French language flourished to such an extent that in her
lifetime Grandmother Landry never learned more than a few
words of English. When Grandfather Landry died, his sons
built Gabrielle's much-loved grandmother a small house in
Somerset, where she lived before coming to die at her daughter's house on Deschambault Street at the age of eighty-four.
The little house in Somerset, built in the French Canadian
style, served as a model for the house described in the story
"My Almighty Grandmother" in *The Road Past Altamont*,
where the narrator enjoys "listening to the lamentations of
the prairie wind as it writhed interminably in the sunlight,
forming and re-forming tiny rings of dust" while sitting
alone with her grandmother, whose wonderful stories led her

granddaughter to believe that it could not possibly have been a male God who created the earth but rather "an old woman with extremely capable hands" (6, 16). So attached was Gabrielle to this house that when the English woman who had purchased it died, Roy journeyed there intent on buying back the property. Although a ruin by that time, the house held so many joyful memories that Roy very nearly bought it anyway.

The decision by the government to build a railroad through Somerset rather than Saint-Léon guaranteed the demise of the latter. Regardless, Roy's love for the past and for her family resides in this area of the Manitoban map. Elie Landry died when Roy was four or five, and Emilie, his wife, died when Roy was eight. Although her memories of her grandmother remained vivid all her life, her Uncle Excide's farm and the nearby prairies dominated remembrances of these beloved summer holidays. As Joan Hind-Smith points out, Roy's youthful memory of the enclosed farmhouse situated in such close proximity to the open plain provides dynamic tension in much of her writing: "On the one hand she longs for the safe, enclosed shelter of family and friends, and on the other she is driven towards the loneliness of achievement" (74).

Uncle Excide, almost a character from a Russian novel with his untamed gaiety giving way in the next instant to bouts of doom and gloom, embodied the pioneering spirit of his parents. He gave up the paternal home in Saint-Léon to build a home nearer to Somerset; the proximity of this English-speaking city was not, however, without its influence on his children, nearly all of whom eventually abandoned their French background, something which caused Roy great pain. Excide became a widower early on when his wife, the former Luzina Major, died of tuberculosis. Beloved of all for her tender heart, this aunt made a profound impression on the young Gabrielle, who later, testifying to her affection, named one of her most memorable characters, Luzina Tousignant of *Where Nests the Water Hen*, after this charming woman. Into this motherless but not at all disorderly household Gabrielle and her mother would arrive, her mother taking over the household chores from her niece, Léa, and Gabrielle riding off on her little roan mare to visit Saint-Léon and its environs for the good of family history and of her soul.

While Excide's pleasant house, with its handpumps that brought water inside from a well and its central heating, pleased Gabrielle, its proximity to a little wood left a much stronger impression on her. As with the "mountain" at Babcock, an actual description of the wood would belie Gabrielle's youthful exaggerated impression of it, but for the young girl, this clump of trees, probably aspen and oak, represented the archetypal forest, welcoming her fanciful imagination and her belief in nature's magic. Once she emerged from the wood at the end of the road to Excide's farm, the prairie called to her. She was mesmerized and deeply moved by the unique beauty of the prairie vista, a wonder evoked many times in the mature Roy's narratives. For example, in the following passage from *The Road Past Altamont*, Christine describes the aspen grove and the prairie at her Uncle Cléophas's farm:

> For as soon as you came out of this wood at my uncle's, you found yourself on the edge of an immense plain, quite open and almost entirely in crops. So that at my uncle's I never knew which I liked best — the grove of aspens that sheltered us, served as a hiding place, and made us feel at home, or the great spread-out land that seemed to summon us to voyages. As my uncle said, both had charm, one reposing from the other. (46)

Indeed boundaries — between wood and field, field and farm, prairie and town, rich and poor — always held a special attraction for Roy, providing as they do a suitable vantage point from which to consider both sides, "one reposing from the other." As she told Donald Cameron, explaining why she did not live with the poor people of Saint-Henri she describes in *The Tin Flute*, preferring instead to reside in a neighbourhood that bordered the rich and poor sections of Montreal, "I have tried to stay always on the borderline, because that's the best place to understand" (135). To adopt one perspective at the expense of the other, she always felt, resulted in overlooking the truth.

In her investigations of Uncle Excide's farm, she eventually discovered another road which led to a slope that offered an even more stirring view of the prairies. Of this discovery, she told no one; she chose to keep secret this special place of solitude, believing as we all do about cherished things that to share them is somehow to dilute their unique powers. The ineffable wonder she felt at the top of the slope, with the immense Manitoba sky above and the expansive plains unfolding below in all their mystery, she interpreted as a promise of joy in her future life.

The enchantment of the land held such power over Roy that later in life during her infrequent visits with the few family members still living in the area, relatives would often complain of her priority first to see places and then to visit people. In truth, places did not let Roy down as frequently as did people. The remoter villages and their surrounding areas compensated somewhat for the disillusionment she felt as the English influence eroded and finally won over much of the French life-style in the larger cities. Family members living in Somerset succumbed to pressures, mainly market driven, by putting up their business signs in English and letting that language finally dominate their whole life. The magnetic attraction of potential economic gain pulled many to large metropolitan areas like Winnipeg, Chicago, and Vancouver — indeed, nearly all of Excide's sons eventually settled in one of these areas. The continued erosion of French life in Manitoba and in other areas wherein the English language dominated came to distress Roy a great deal. In 1976, she told David Cobb that even Saint-Boniface looked English from the outside, adding that "I dare not say it, but French there now seems to be only a matter of culture, not of life" (10). Consequently, trips to Somerset later in life discouraged Roy more and more; while her uncle lived, however, she could be certain of finding replenishment and nourishment for her French ways at Excide's farm.

The power of the contentment and joy Roy found at her uncle's is best explained by an incident that took place during the year she taught at Cardinal, only a few miles north of Somerset. Roy recreates the atmosphere of Cardinal in *Children of My Heart* and in the final chapter of *Street of Riches* — the city is painted all in red but for the little white school in which Christine teaches — although neither work describes the village in great detail (apparently Roy could not bear to evoke it in its entirety). Probably already suffering from ill-defined resentment at being the teacher her mother wanted her to become instead of the writer she herself desired to be, Roy felt overwhelmingly homesick in this unliveliest of places. Its proximity to Excide's, on the other hand, allowed a happy change of scenery and of personality. Confined by her role as a proper schoolmistress during the weekdays, Roy cut loose almost every weekend at her uncle's. A fifteen-minute train ride deposited her Saturday mornings in Somerset, where invariably she would meet one of her cousins come to town to shop; sometimes when her uncle had business in Cardinal (he liked the work of a blacksmith / mechanic there), he would collect Roy on Friday evenings. The Landry house offered everything Cardinal did not: laughter, song, dance, fellowship. In the comfort of a centrally heated house, Roy could wash her hair without fear of catching a chill from the cold, an important consideration given her health problems; she and Léa would play duets together, collapsing in laughter over some of the piano's idiosyncrasies; and here, too, Roy committed numerous faux pas by her inattentiveness to the attentions of certain village swains. At Uncle Excide's, Roy was, in other words, anything but the depressed European traveller in search of herself or the solitude-seeking and at times antisocial writer she would later become. Instead, she was irreverent, cavalier, frivolous, teasing, a startling contrast to the serious, sober young teacher at Cardinal, who, from the sidelines, wondered at the emptiness of the lives of her village's inhabitants. She captures the distressed tone of those lives in certain sections of *Children of My Heart*, especially those dealing with the hard-hearted, ignorant, and alcoholic Eymard, who tries to sully the love his maturing son, Médéric, feels for his teacher.

The weekends at Excide's continued throughout the harsh prairie winter Roy spent at Cardinal, transportation sometimes coming in the form of sleigh rides with a horse that actually knew the way. Saturday and Sunday banished Roy's loneliness, endowing her with the necessary courage to survive the next five days, after which she would return to the farm, her coping gauge running on empty, ready for life as it should be lived. In March, nature intruded on Gabrielle's sanctuary, the same hostile nature so vividly portrayed in *Where Nests the Water Hen* during Luzina's journey with the morose and unsociable Nick Sluzick to give birth to her last child. Rain melted the snow, and the mild weather turned the countryside into a morass of mud and muck, making travel to and from Excide's nearly impossible. A couple of weekends cooped up in Cardinal proved too much for Gabrielle; intrepid to a fault, Roy, limited by her experiences of surviving winters in the city, convinced herself one day that the ground had dried sufficiently for her to venture a walk from the train station to her uncle's farm.

The beginning of the adventure proved rather comic, for Roy arrived at Somerset by handcar, which was little more than an exposed platform powered along the rails by pumping a lever up and down. Stepping off the platform at a section of road that led to the shortest route, Roy faced a vacant countryside full of ooze and water. Water, a classic obstacle to overcome in so many Romance quests, proved just that; even a warning not to cross a small stream shouted by an unknown denizen of a nearby house could not deter our heroine. Gamely but tentatively, Roy forded her first obstacle, as if by magic finding exactly the right footing to keep the water below the level of her knee-high boots. From there, by keeping close to the road, Roy was able to make some progress — until she decided to take a shortcut through part of the woods near her uncle's that even as children they had always avoided.

The sun's setting even as her fatigue from pulling sodden boots from the sucking mud increased, she could not resist the temptation of taking what seemed the easier path. At first confident as the cooling air added firmness to the ground, she suddenly found herself up to her hips in a pit of freezing muck. Near panic, she could only crawl out of this dangerous trap, for the edges of the hole collapsed with the slightest pressure and made standing impossible. She soon realized that the trail had led her onto a pond covered with a treacherous, thin layer of ice that collapsed under her weight. On her stomach, Roy half crawled, half swam to some nearby trees. The rains fell; coyotes howled in the distance.

Only a few yards from her haven, she realized to her despair that going any farther meant death; she would have to retrace her path of full-length body imprints across the same section of the pond in order to reach the road, a surer but much longer way to shelter. Love, warm and comforting behind the closed doors of Excide's house, could not rescue her. As she battled against death, Gabrielle felt its unfair cruelty since those she loved most, so near and yet so far away, remained unaware of her plight. But perhaps love saved her after all. Cold, exhausted, disheartened, Roy refused to give up. Laboriously retracing her previous route, crawling, pulling herself along on her stomach, she eventually reached the road. In a nightmare of rain and ice and battling the desire to sleep, after five hours of "shortcuts," Roy arrived at the house, knocked, and fell into the arms of her astonished relatives. From then on, someone turned up almost every week to escort Roy back to what sustained her. As she wrote, commenting on this life-threatening incident some forty years later, "We'll move heaven and earth to return to where we've been happy, even if it costs us our last breath" (*Enchantment* 96).

PERILS OF PROGRESS

One of the pleasures of reading Gabrielle Roy's books lies in the discovery of statements, gems like the one that concludes the preceding paragraph, about the human condition. The reader can find much solace in such statements, finely honed by a keen observer of daily life who finds the words to express cogently what one may feel only confusedly or vaguely. In *The Hidden Mountain*, the artist Pierre Cadorai, during his Atlantic crossing, finds himself one day in the ship's library leafing through an edition of the complete works of William Shakespeare. Haphazardly, according to the narrator, he stumbles across the following passage from *Hamlet*:

If thou didst ever hold me in thy heart,
Absent thee from felicity awhile,
And in this harsh world draw thy breath in pain,
To tell my story. (116)

Pierre meditates over this passage, particularly its final four words, believing that Shakespeare here touches on one of the profound desires of all humans: to have their story told, that someone could care enough about another to remember and to relate a little of what that life was about. And through writing, perhaps, to make that life indelible, even immortal.

Despite her ability to shape her own story in her autobiography or to create the lives of others in her narratives, Roy would be the first to admit the lack of control she, like anyone else, exerted over her own life. Thus, for all the happiness Uncle Excide's farm held for Roy, this happiness was subject to the forces of change. For all of the wisdom her books provide, Roy found translating that wisdom into the workings of her own life a daunting task at times. In the case of Excide's farm, Roy tried to go back years later to recapture some of the wonder the much younger Gabrielle had felt. Like so many of the characters in her works, Roy herself often yearned to recover the idealized days of childhood. We all know the adage "You can't go back," but such knowledge cannot always shield us from disappointment. We have already seen how she wished to buy her beloved Grandmother Landry's former house in Somerset, dilapidated though it was. In midlife, during one of her trips back to Manitoba from her permanent residence in Quebec, Roy visited Excide's eldest son, the only one who had stayed in the area. Thanks to advancements in farming technology, Roy's cousin could reside in his modern, ranch-style home in the nearby village and maintain his father's land single-handedly, a job that previously required a corps of labourers. This change alone made Roy feel that she had stepped into another world, the normal cacophony of a busy farm replaced by the low hum of a single tractor's engine. The perfect order of a farm run by a man who clocked in and out like a factory worker impressed Roy, but nothing hinted at the dramatic change "progress" had worked on the house, which represented happiness incarnate in Roy's childhood. Peering through one of the windows, Roy was unprepared for the hurt that assailed her — the ceiling removed and the inside walls torn down, the house, now a shed, sheltered the huge tractor. Nothing substantive at all remained of the place that had formerly extended her the best of life: fun, lightheartedness, freedom from the daily woes of Saint-Boniface and Cardinal, all adding up to true peace of mind for a tormented young soul. Comfort from her upset came in a subsequent visit to her grandparents' gravestones. Remembering their accomplishments renewed the bond she felt for these industrious although not very happy pioneers. Nearby, Roy found the plot for her Uncle Excide and Aunt Luzina. Poor Gabrielle, her relatives' gravestones boldly spelled out their ultimate loss to her: "Father" and "Mother," not in French but in English! Two people who had never been so addressed during their lifetimes and who embodied for Roy the richness of her French cultural heritage had been erased from her life more definitely than on the day each died. Equally important, but far more pathetic, "Mother" and "Father" erased the essence of Excide's and Luzina's true lives from human history. Resurrected though they might briefly be thanks to the talents of their author-niece, their story represents the sad tale of loss, of life's ephemeral nature.

Although hardly against change, Roy nevertheless maintains throughout her nonfiction and her fiction an ambivalent attitude toward "progress." Thus, while the young Roy marvels at her Uncle Excide's central heating or at her cousin's powerful tractor, the mature woman laments the dominance of English in her relatives' lives. Even in 1942, in "The Hutterites," an article written for *Le bulletin des agriculteurs*, Roy applauds the social system of the communal immigrants where personal possessions are unheard of. She notes that the "motivation of personal gain may not play a role in their case, but this does not exclude a desire for progress" (*Fragile* 24); and yet, although she does not share all the sect's beliefs, she expresses worry over the good that will be lost due to this desired progress:

> I went on my way, reassured about the curiosity of the young Hutterites, which will surely lead them out of their isolation. But at the same time I was afraid.
> *"Please God they do not lose because of coming to us."*
> (*Fragile* 29; our emphasis)

Roy's concern over the cost exacted by change, in the name of almighty progress, is a recurring motif in her works, particularly in *Windflower*, which offers a somewhat tragic, although at times also humorous, look at the incursion of Western civilization or "progress" into the Arctic world. Even the upbeat introduction Roy wrote for *Man and His World* to commemorate the 1967 world fair in Montreal — an essay which for the most part expresses great hope in the gifts promised by progress and especially technology, words often uttered in the same breath — contains a caveat. Noting that "progress does not always have a gentle face," Roy warns that it "often gives rise to its own adversary": among other things, "egotism, . . . our cruel indifference toward misfortunes, and repulsive racial pride so contrary to our advancement" (*Fragile* 216). Indeed, few visits to past places of refuge gave her more pleasure than her return to the Water Hen district, where she discovered that the islands were no longer populated, that "progress" had retreated from the area, leaving it even more pristine than she remembered.

Loss, recuperation, life's joys and sorrows, memories lovingly transfigured by nostalgia, years, and distance — in 1927, upon graduation from high school, Roy was already well acquainted with these motifs, whose significance later experiences often reaffirmed. Already oversensitive at times to life's demands, even at graduation Roy imagined a future tinged not with idealistic expectations but hung over with dark clouds. An ageing father, an exigent mother, and a three-storey house on rue Deschambault looked to her for financial support.

During the first two decades of Gabrielle's life, her mother had only scoffed at her precocious interest in writing and later at her literary aspirations. Her seeking refuge during childhood and adolescence in the attic where she spent hours dreaming, reading the old books stored there, and writing about her uncles provided the young author with some solace. From the age of ten, she wrote plays in which she enlisted the neighbourhood children to perform. To Joan Hind-Smith, Gabrielle related a humorous anecdote about one play in particular, a murder mystery with the memorable line, "There lies the rotting carcass." The boy who spoke the line, Louis, had apparently recited it to his horrified mother, who forbade him to use the words. Well, when the young author learned what had happened, she accosted Louis, demanding, "Who is the author of this play, your mother or me?" Duly chastised, Louis afterwards recited the lines exactly as Gabrielle had written them. Thus, as Hind-Smith notes, "Gabrielle had defended the inviolable rights of the author at an early age" (72–73). At eleven, she began the novel in which she portrayed her uncles in ways that met with Mélina's wrath; her mother burned the pages in the stove. Impervious apparently in only this one area to her daughter's needs, Mélina's thoughts extended no further than to keeping Gabrielle by her and securing for her daughter a steady job that would ease some of the family's financial straits.

FIGURE 11

The Roy family in 1912. Back row, from left to right: Bernadette, Clémence, Adèle, Anna, and Rodolphe. Front row: Léon, Germain, Gabrielle, and Mélina. Joseph, the eldest, is not pictured.

Although Roy threads details of her mother's unceasing obsession with money throughout much of her autobiography, she makes no mention there of her early literary endeavours, an omission that testifies to her conflicted feelings about her mother. The omission also emphasizes the fact that Gabrielle did not write for awhile after the book burning, not so much because she feared her mother but because she feared failure.

Roy spent the second half of her life trying to forgive herself for not returning to Saint-Boniface after her return from Europe. The claustrophobic conditions awaiting her there repelled her as much as her indebtedness to her mother demanded reciprocal self-sacrifice on her part. Mélina brooked no choice in her daughter's vocation except for the vocation of teacher; she saw her daughter's artistic aspirations as pipe dreams that guaranteed continued poverty. Despite the economic hardship Gabrielle's completion of grade twelve meant for the Roys, Gabrielle's mother had pulled off a financial miracle; Gabrielle graduated and would continue her education in hopes, at least from her mother's perspective, of securing a teaching job that would keep her close to home. Unable to rebel until later with half a continent separating her from Mélina, Roy, like her fictional soulmate Christine in *Street of Riches*, dutifully began her college studies. In 1927, financed by the academic awards she had earned in high school, she entered the Anglophone world of Winnipeg Normal Institute, having been preceded there by her older sisters Anna and Adèle.

SISTERS AND BROTHERS

Gabrielle Roy's seven siblings — Joseph, Anna, Adèle, Rodolphe, Bernadette, Clémence, and Germain — were all older than Gabrielle, and each one affected her life to a different degree. Mélina Roy apparently had three other children, who all died young, only two of whom Gabrielle ever mentions: Agnès, who died at fourteen, and Marie-Agnès, who died at four years of age. The second Agnès, who was killed in a fire, adored her brand new sister, Gabrielle, even trying at times to hide the baby from Mélina so that she could be the mother. Most of what we know about these brothers and sisters derives from glimpses found in Gabrielle's correspondence, wherein it becomes clear that all her siblings equalled their younger sister in sensitivity, although none equalled her in artistic talent. As Gabrielle herself observed in a letter to her cloistered sister Bernadette, "All of us — all Mélina's children — have a tendency to live too much on our nerves. It makes the fire burn bright, true enough, but later we pay for it dearly, don't we?" (3 Dec. 1961, *Letters* 43).

Roy's brothers seem to have made the least impression on her life. Joseph, born in 1887, the eldest of the Roy children, led what Gabrielle characterized as a "vagabond existence" (*Enchantment* 107). In the habit of disappearing for years at a time, he eventually settled down later in life, married, and had children. Gabrielle spent a few weeks with her oldest brother and his wife, the former Julia Marquis, in the summer of 1951, probably the last time she saw Joseph before his death in 1956. Jos, as he was called, and Julia lived in Dollard, Saskatchewan, one of the many villages founded by Roy's father when he worked as a settlement agent for the federal government. There Léon not only settled French Canadians from Quebec and the United States but also left part of his heart; he spoke frequently about Dollard to his family, which may account for some of his children settling there. Anna and her husband, Albert, lived in Dollard at the beginning of their marriage, and Germain taught there for a while. During Roy's visit with Jos and his wife, she grew to appreciate Julia, admiring in parti-cular her generosity, tenderness, humanity, and especially her extraordinary devotion to a man with whom living was hardly easy. Jos, ailing and anxious, seemed always on the verge of a horrible asthma attack. Julia and Jos apparently suited each other, both of them being somewhat brusque in manner. Like his youngest sister, Jos took great enjoyment from sitting on the front porch of his house in Saskatchewan, watching the horizon and the small hills which gave some relief from the flat plains. The sunsets there were particularly stunning, their reds unlike anything Gabrielle had seen anywhere. The memory of the sunsets and the view from Jos's porch, inextricably linked to many others, guided her thoughts in writing the story "The Road Past Altamont," in the collection of stories by that same title.

Rodolphe, born in 1899, the sixth of the Roy children and Gabrielle's godfather, was the most exciting and outgoing of them all, the life-of-the-party personality with all its attendant joys and sorrows. A song forever on his lips, he could bang out an air from *Rigoletto* by ear on the old piano or stir up his family with some rollicking song. A free spirit, a gambler, a loser, usually tipsy, he would blow into town and expansively hand out ten-dollar and fifty-dollar notes along with praise and empty promises. Affectionate and spontaneous, Rodolphe knew no greater enemy than himself; after solving his mother's financial crises on one day, the following he would ask back his handouts and even solicit a little loan to see him through. Unfortunately, as he grew older, Rodolphe's sense of fun led him down the road to gambling and alcoholism. As a young man not without talent, he had worked as a telegraphist and then as a stationmaster; when posted near Saint-Boniface during those years, he visited often with his family. After losing his job during the Depression, Rodolphe confronted the same situation as the poor described in *The Tin Flute*, and on the advent of World War II he enlisted to receive a steady paycheque as a soldier. (Of all the Roy children, only Gabrielle enjoyed full-time employment during the Depression, which accounts in part for the family's negative reaction to her leaving for Europe when she did.) Never marrying, Rodolphe spent his last years among questionable friends in Vancouver, looked after from time to time by Jos's son, Robert Roy. Fortunately, Mélina did not live long enough to witness the deterioration of his final years. For a period of time, he completely alienated Gabrielle, behind her back attempting to borrow money from her friends, acquaintances, her husband, and even her husband's sister. She eventually forgave such follies, but news from him or about him in her later life upset her deeply, and so as much as possible she kept her distance. Bernadette and Anna visited Rodolphe in spring 1963 at Powell River in British Columbia, where he worked in a motel. Although they responded to his cry for help that turned out to be crying wolf, the loving Bernadette faithfully visited her older brother again from the end of December 1969 until mid-January 1970. He died on 28 June 1971 in his tiny apartment in Vancouver; his door was unlocked as always, in case he needed help from a buddy during an asthma attack, and he was found with his pockets picked.

Germain, the most "normal" of the eight children, died tragically in 1961 at the age of fifty-nine from injuries sustained in a car accident in Saint-Boniface. A teacher, as were all of his sisters except Clémence, Germain left home as soon as he could to avoid being a financial burden to his mother, taking his first job at the local Collège de Saint-Boniface, where he worked twenty-four hours a week for his room and board and a few dollars. During Germain's year at the college, his wife Antonia, also a teacher, lived on her own with their two-year-old daughter, teaching in a remote area for the pathetic sum of sixty dollars a month, a salary no one would have dared offer a man. Germain then obtained a teaching position in Saskatchewan (Gabrielle lent him the $19.50 ticket fare) not far from where his wife worked, allowing them to see each other on weekends. Germain and Antonia, after many, many years and a second daughter, finally realized their forgivable dream of working together in the same school, he as principal and she as an elementary teacher. Money must have remained a concern for them since, in 1948, Gabrielle decided to help their elder daughter, Lucille, to attend medical school. Of the two daughters, the younger one, Yolande, who at this writing resides in Ottawa, remained the most faithful to the French way of life, greatly pleasing her famous aunt by travelling to France in 1962, sure to be "Frenchified" by the experience; on the other hand, Gabrielle was nonplussed when she learned that Lucille spoke English even to her children. Gabrielle obviously made some effort to keep up with the lives of her brothers and their children. And while she did not return to Saint-Boniface for Germain's funeral, she did visit him in the hospital, where he consoled his little sister by recognizing and smiling at her when she entered, and where they had a last chance to talk together. Roy's memories of all her siblings seem always to turn to their manner of death; the youngest of the eight who survived to be adults, Gabrielle outlived them all.

Did the sisters fare better than their brothers? Standing back to get a broader perspective on this generation of Roys, one cannot help but feel that most of them fell victim to their own extreme sensitivity, a beautiful flame that rendered their joys all the more keen but also made their suffering equally acute. Gabrielle writes that, in comparison with her brothers and sisters, she was perhaps the only sibling with the capacity for happiness, a gaiety that endeared her to her mother. Indeed, Mélina's one lifelong sorrow was that her children were not happy. Even Gabrielle was not insulated from the complications that beset her sisters' respective lives, particularly during the second half of her life when she lived in Quebec and consciously maintained her distance from the family.

Mélina especially grieved for both Anna, born the year after Joseph in 1888, and for Adèle, born after Anna in 1892. Anna became a teacher, and at the age of nineteen she married Albert Painchaud (whose delicious name translates into "warm bread"). Her mother's sorrow derived from watching her passionate and intelligent daughter marry too young and below herself. While to all appearances Albert was a good and loving man and a good provider, he matched his wife neither in sensitivity nor in education. Of Anna, Gabrielle writes: "I often remember seeing her stand motionless at a window, gazing out but seeing nothing, as though knowing she'd been destined for better things and it was now too late" (*Enchantment* 106). Wherever Anna's remarkable talents could have led her, marriage channelled them into a stultifying dead end. And whatever love Anna longed for, she got only on her deathbed, her frustrating, demanding nature having always alienated those from whom she desired love the most. Life must, however, have brought her some cheer with the births of three sons, Fernand (born the same year as his aunt Gabrielle), Paul, and Gilles. In addition, she and her husband eventually built a lovely home, affectionately called "Painchaudière," which became one of the cherished gathering places of the Roy family, in Saint-Vital (where Gabrielle was later married), next to Saint-Boniface along the Red River. But material success did not bring happiness.

In May 1947, in the midst of all the hubbub surrounding the publication of her first book, Gabrielle found time for the first time in four years (since her mother's death in 1943) to travel west. She visited with the convalescing Anna, who had just returned home to Painchaudière from a hospital stay. During this same visit, Gabrielle met Marcel Carbotte for the first time; three months later the two married. Despite the triumph such a visit must have meant to the now famous author, Gabrielle's chief concern in a letter to her sister Bernadette, written on 10 May 1947, is the mentally ill Clémence, whose special needs would be a source of worry for many years to come. As with so many of her future visits to Manitoba, illness or some other urgency generally motivated her return to the places and to the people whose memories inspired so much of what she wrote.

Anna and Albert sold their home in Saint-Vital in 1961. Gabrielle immediately sent Anna some Equanil, a mild tranquillizer, fearing the consequences of such a move on their health and their psyches. As with the sale of the house on rue Deschambault, overseen by Gabrielle prior to her leaving for Europe, the loss of Painchaudière in a sense cast the siblings adrift once again. In the end, however, Albert's decision to sell the house, as well as to liquidate his affairs, proved timely since he died that October. Like Luzina, although by no means as content as the fictional mother in *Where Nests the Water Hen*, Anna afterwards spent her time visiting her grown children.

For a while she lived with her eldest, Fernand, and his wife, Léontine, in Saint-Vital. Her husband having left her fairly well-heeled financially, Anna travelled a lot from 1961 to 1963, staying with her son Paul in Marmora, Ontario, and with her sister, Adèle, in Montreal. She eventually spent time with her youngest, Gilles, in Cornwall, Pennsylvania, and travelled with Bernadette to visit Rodolphe in British Columbia, all this time using Winnipeg as a sort of home base. In October 1963, Anna moved, for the last time, to join Fernand and Léontine, who had settled in Arizona. There, cancer of the intestine, which had dogged her for fifteen years, finally caught up with her. Gabrielle, who lamented that most of her trips west were to attend funerals, spent the last two weeks of Anna's life at her bedside. Anna told Gabrielle of her lacklustre life, of her feeling of not having had her fair share, a feeling corrob-orated by Gabrielle, who describes her eldest sister as "having floundered right and left, grasping desperately for a little happiness" (*Enchantment* 129).

In her own way, and despite her prickly nature, Anna must have cared for her youngest sister. In listing the people Gabrielle wishes she could bring back to life to share her moments of triumph — her father to tell him that she finished top in her class at teacher's college and her mother to tell her all the wonderful things that happened to her since the publication of her first novel — she includes Anna. Gabrielle wished she could tell Anna, who had worried how love, mar-riage, and family ties — those very things that seem not to have brought Anna happiness — would affect her baby sister, that "those shackles had in fact been rather good for me" (*Enchantment* 81). In that same paragraph in her autobiography, Gabrielle also regrets the loss of another sister, Bernadette. In reference to "Dédette" she writes, "Nowadays it's Dédette I keep calling to in vain, wanting so much to tell her it's all right about a particular sorrow in my life, the one she knew about and was so upset by" (81). Although Roy could refer to any number of sadnesses that afflicted her life, our interpretation of the evidence leads us to name a specific heartache: Adèle.

FIGURE 12

Adèle (left), Gabrielle, and Bernadette in 1914.

ADÈLE AND GABRIELLE

Was Adèle tragic or just plain nasty? Did she feel unable to change the course of her own ruined life, and therefore try to wreak as much havoc as she could on the lives of others, including her famous sibling? Was she unable to forgive her sister for using an intimate detail from her life as the basis for a short story? Was she jealous of a fame she believed circumstances cheated her of and that by all rights should have been hers? None of the above? All of the above?

In *Street of Riches*, first published as *Rue Deschambault* in Montreal in 1955, Roy included the short story "To Prevent a Marriage," told from the first-person perspective of a little girl. In this tale, the girl and her mother travel to Saskatchewan to prevent her older sister Georgianna's marriage at too young an age to a boy whom the parents consider no good. The mother and Georgianna argue, the latter insisting, "I love him; I'm going to get married" (*Street* 44). But Georgianna's love story and the marriage to come are secondary elements in the narrative. Roy devotes most of her talents instead to capturing the innocent child's impressions of the trip and her resulting adventures. In real life, Gabrielle's sister, the beautiful, lovely Adèle, did marry disastrously, finding herself single again almost immediately; whether from shame or anguish or simply as an attempt to put the past behind her, she moved farther and farther away from Saint-Boniface. In "To Prevent a Marriage," the fictive mother offers a prophetic warning to Georgianna, who insists that she will marry for love: " 'Poor Georgianna,' Maman then exclaimed, 'you talk of love as though it would last. . . . But when it goes . . . if there is nothing to take its place . . . it's horrible!' " (45). Certainly the bitter Adèle might have read a painful truth into these words and in her paranoia seen them as a personal attack of some kind.

As with the other Roy children, Adèle was sensitive, bright, adventuresome, but complex. Gabrielle's godmother and fifteen years her senior, Adèle taught school in the far reaches of Alberta and often returned during the summer holidays. Adèle's fad diets (nothing but spinach, lemons, and apples one year, prunes and oatmeal the next, and citrus fruits, nuts, and dates a third summer) could be symptomatic of many things: weight-consciousness, or attempts at better health through better diet, or, perhaps, an eating disorder triggered by low self-esteem. One summer, when Adèle ate too quickly through her cache of special foods for her current diet, she ended up at the table eating like the rest of the family. "[This was] one of the rare times she deigned to behave like everybody else," comments Gabrielle (*Enchantment* 101). Adèle seemed never to fit in with her family or anywhere else, feeling at odds with the world around her, and the family explained away the troubled woman's behaviour after her failed marriage as that of someone on the run. She would find a teaching job in one of what the family characterized as "Adèle's hardship villages," would stay for a year or two until life became a little easier, and then, perhaps fearful or feeling herself undeserving of peace or happiness, would move again, farther north, farther away (*Enchantment* 106). Although all the family members suffered in one form or another from what Gabrielle frequently called "the travelling sickness," Adèle's constant shifting indicated serious problems. According to Gabrielle, seemingly rootless, Adèle had little aptitude for adapting herself to others; she lacked the flexibility needed to keep human interrelationships running at all smoothly, and she drove away the people she needed the most. Even in the years before her own death, when her attitude toward the troubled woman who had so vexed her life had softened, Roy's interpretation of Adèle's behaviour more closely resembles a clinical evaluation than an honest vindication:

> I realize now that she craved affection and longed to be understood and accepted, but everything she did seemed designed to rebuff affection. I've often wondered if people like Adèle are incapable of reaching out to others because there's no love in their lives, or

whether their inability to reach out has kept love at bay. (*Enchantment* 101)

Over time, Gabrielle became a chief focus of Adèle's ill will. By 1962, Gabrielle mentions in a letter to Bernadette that Adèle had returned, via Clémence, Gabrielle's gift of $100. At this point Gabrielle knew that Adèle harboured feelings of rancour against her but did not have any clear idea why. When Gabrielle sent this awkward sister another $100 for Christmas, Adèle again failed to cash the cheque, either out of vengeance or a desire to punish Gabrielle. And while Gabrielle admitted that she may have wronged Adèle at one time or another, she saw these wrongs as no more or less than those that occur normally in interactions between people. She felt that Adèle's behaviour was childish and that her sense of persecution blew everything out of proportion.

By the end of the 1960s, Adèle began to use her famous sister's name as a means of entrance into various circles, particularly publishing houses. Once admitted, Adèle spoke ill of Gabrielle, blaming her for all kinds of things, thinking in a perverse way to further her own goals. For Adèle was a writer, too. From what Gabrielle heard, Adèle used her sister's name to get her own work accepted for consideration for publication. The publishers were, they told Gabrielle, reluctant to refuse Adèle's work in her presence, so insistent, even threatening, was her behaviour. When her work was inevitably rejected, adding fuel to her already roaring rancour, she either berated the publishers in person or wrote them abusive letters. As Gabrielle wrote to Bernadette, Adèle gained little by using her name, even less by putting her sister down; one's work either stands on its own merits or faces rejection.

At a small party with friends and publishers, Gabrielle eventually learned of a particular manuscript of Adèle's that could not find a publisher: a mean-spirited, tell-all tale about Gabrielle Roy, worthy not even of the tawdriest tabloid. That a vindictive and unfair account of her life had circulated among all the Montreal publishers and even some in the

United States cut Gabrielle deeply; that her sister Adèle was the author caused Gabrielle much anxiety. Ironically, an unwitting Gabrielle had earlier wished her sister all kinds of success for her enormous effort in composing this manuscript. The secret contents of the manuscript now exposed, the numerous rejections Adèle received explained themselves. We can only surmise that, while the much-rejected text may not have been without some interest, it was probably laced with a vindictive, bitter, too personal tone of vengeance. After learning the truth about the manuscript in October 1968, Roy surmised that Adèle had probably nursed such an endeavour for many, many years, dating back to 1955, when, in a letter, Anna had alerted Gabrielle that her godmother was up to no good. Indeed, Gabrielle believed that Anna's presence somehow delayed Adèle's putting pen to paper. Obviously, Adèle wasted no time in realizing this project after Anna's death in 1964.

The incident responsible for the breach between the sisters probably dates back to the early 1950s, although the seeds for such an estrangement were perhaps even sown years earlier. When Gabrielle made known her decision to leave for Europe in 1937, Adèle, who clearly tended toward theatrical extremes, accused her of betraying her people; behind Gabrielle's back, Adèle raged at their mother for having spoiled her youngest daughter, for having pampered and indulged her only to reap her ingratitude. If Adèle's motivation derived purely from her sister's perceived lack of consideration for others, then jealousy certainly must have raised its ugly head when her own book, *Le pain de chez nous: histoire d'une famille manitobaine*, published in 1954, was easily superseded in quality and in sales by Gabrielle's *Rue Deschambault*, published in 1955, which was also based on their family history and contained the story "To Prevent a Marriage." Gabrielle's book, translated into English as *Street of Riches*, won her a second Governor General's Award for Fiction in 1957 as well as the French Prix Duvernay in 1956, an award that honoured both this particular novel and her overall contribution to literature.

Clearly the presence of Adèle's hurtful manuscript making the rounds of publishing houses disrupted Roy's tranquil life, and convinced her of Adèle's implacable hatred, of her mental instability, and of her intent to do harm. For a long time she did not even tell her husband about this troubling matter. From what she could learn of the manuscript, its story line centred solely on a very inward-looking Adèle, the blameless and much-persecuted central character, while denigrating those around her, apparently offering nothing of general interest but only her own twisted point of view. The book did, however, include one authentic document whose context Adèle twisted to her own pathetic ends, an intimate letter from Gabrielle to her sister in which she opened up her heart to a reader she assumed was on her side. When Adèle could bring herself to focus on something other than her own paranoia and assumed persecution, she seems to have enjoyed at least a modicum of success. Writing under the name Marie-Anna Roy, she followed *Le pain de chez nous* with *Valcourt; ou La dernière étape: roman du grand nord canadien* (1958), *La Montagne Pembina au temps des colons: historique des paroisses de la région de la Montagne Pembina et biographies des principaux pionniers* (1969), *Les visages du vieux Saint-Boniface* (1970), *Les capuchins de Toutes-aides* (1977), and *Le miroir du passé* (1979).

Adèle finally deposited her manuscript under the pseudonym Irma Deloy or Deroy in a Quebec university, having previously hinted at her intention to do so when she visited her niece, Yolande (Germain's daughter), in 1968. One can only speculate as to why the university library director accepted these pages in the first place. Gabrielle learned, from a professor friend of hers who taught at this university and who had seen the manuscript, that anyone who wished could consult it. Having been unsuccessful in her attempts to publish it, Adèle at least had the satisfaction of knowing it was available publicly, a happy conclusion to a malice carefully contemplated and artfully prepared over many years to torture her despised sister. And she certainly stabbed her younger sister in a vulnerable spot, for Gabrielle seems to have worried a great deal about maintaining a positive reputation amongst her reading public. All forms of criticism hurt this highly sensitive woman, who not only guarded her privacy but was also aware that she represented a minority voice in a profession dominated by men. The professor in question, who was researching a thesis on the Canadian novel, telephoned Gabrielle for an interview, offering to show her the manuscript in his possession. He went on to describe the work as an ugly and hate-filled attack against Gabrielle and offered to write an article to refute its false claims. Roy refused flatly to read what Adèle had written and argued against a refutation, reasoning that such an article would only draw more attention than merited to the trash her sister had written and give it an importance it did not deserve. (It is fortunate that Adèle did not live in the 1990s, when books that viciously attack celebrities need be neither well written nor truthful; Adèle's vitriol would certainly have found a publisher.) Even Bernadette tried to intervene; she wrote to Adèle from her convent, entreating her to take back the manuscript and to destroy it. Adèle refused, and her response led to a complete falling out with yet another sister.

Whatever the demons that drove Adèle, they found a satisfying and very public target in Gabrielle. One can imagine Gabrielle's anguish during this period of her life: paranoia about what secrets Adèle may have exposed, concern about the effects on her reputation, frustration from her own powerlessness to control the situation. Eventually, through the intercession of influential friends, the university archives locked away the odious manuscript, promising that it would no longer be accessible to anyone. As Gabrielle perceptively worried in a letter to Bernadette, however, the potential for harm remains as long as the text remains; some researcher somewhere in pursuit of the sensational, under the protective aegis of "literary history," would find a way to get at the story. And to complicate matters during this trying time, two photocopies were being circulated, one making its way finally to Bernadette.

FIGURE 13

*Adèle, Clémence, Anna, and Gabrielle in 1943.
The woman to Gabrielle's right is unknown.*

That Gabrielle became the focus of all that went wrong in Adèle's life makes sense in light of the older sister's own literary aspirations. Adèle's contemptible attempt to destroy her sister's reputation in favour of her own seems even more odd when one remembers that by 1968 Adèle was seventy-six years old. Typical of too many highly intelligent and high-strung women in the not distant past with no real or satisfying career to fill their lives, Adèle probably was more than a little unbalanced or "kooky," flitting about from one job to another, travelling some, surrounding herself with eccentric friends. That she never married again nor had children is immaterial; indeed, that she did neither is probably a blessing. Adèle must elicit some sympathy as the gifted-woman-turned-pathetic-drifter because life accorded her no outlets for her talents. However, one's sympathy evaporates for the woman who impinged on Gabrielle's life; Adèle's harm was well defined and intentional. Gabrielle suffered from Adèle's attacks, and that no woman in Roy's fiction possesses the extremely negative traits embodied in this sister may well testify to the pain Adèle inflicted.

CARING FOR CLÉMENCE

Clémence Roy, born in 1895 three years after Adèle, spent her life either dependent on other people, such as her mother and various sisters, or in mental institutions. This tragic figure lived with Mélina until her mother's death in 1943; after that date, Anna and Bernadette took her in tow. Much of Clémence's story concerns attempts to find this troubled person a suitable institution or suitable living situation in which she would be both well cared for and happy, a difficult combination in any case but especially bothersome in Clémence's. Initially, Anna, the eldest, "inherited" Clémence, often picking her up at her little room where she lived alone to bring her, for a few days at a time, to Anna's beautiful property at Saint-Vital. Anna, at fifty-five, was not in good health herself, but the two would shop and otherwise entertain themselves

— happy occasions that made all the sisters recall the "old" Clémence and, despite repeated incidents, hope for a recovery — until Clémence invariably slipped into gloom and silence. No one really knew much about Clémence's disorder, but the sisters did their best to cope with the disheartening situation. During this time, Gabrielle was living hand to mouth in Montreal, absorbed in trying to establish herself as a writer, soothing her conscience over Clémence by her confidence in Anna and by promises to herself that eventually she would be able to help Anna. After the success of The Tin Flute, Gabrielle indeed helped Anna, not emotionally, but financially; in one letter to Bernadette, she promises a cheque for $1,000, to be shared among her sisters (13 June 1949, Letters 15). In the same letter, written in 1949, she wishes that Adèle would move to Manitoba to look after Clémence; one can only speculate about Adèle's reaction had she learned of her youngest sister's idea. Ultimately, the sisters' only option was to institutionalize Clémence in a succession of homes around Saint-Boniface.

Gabrielle had feared that Anna, on her deathbed in early 1964, would bequeath Clémence to her. Anna, however, about a year before, had placed the ill sister under Bernadette's care, much to Gabrielle's private relief. Gabrielle never ceased to worry or to feel guilty about Clémence and was heavily indebted to Anna and Bernadette for relieving her of this unwelcome responsibility. Gabrielle's letters to Bernadette almost choke with her gratitude for her looking after this unfortunate soul. Reading between the lines where Gabrielle is all admiration and praise for her sister's willingness to help, one senses not only Gabrielle's attempts to assuage her own guilt but also her intense relief at being able to depend on someone of Bernadette's ilk, a cloistered nun, dedicated anyway to a life of serving others. When Gabrielle writes in 1943 that their mother left Clémence to the sisters as "a guarantee of salvation, of redemption," in order that they know the blessing of sacrifice, such a statement borders on the unfair (15 September 1943, Letters 4). By acknowledging and honouring her sisters' sacrifices, she diverts attention from her own lack of contribution. As Gabrielle knew too well, writing took her away from her family. Her family, however, took her away from her writing, for which she required long periods of solitude — solitude and separation, as she put the matter, which allowed her to know her family better. Her solution was to send cheques and letters long distance from Quebec.

In the early stages of Clémence's illness during her youth, Mélina would keep her home from school; in this way, it fell to Clémence to look after the baby Gabrielle. The two became very close, taking long walks on the "wild side of our little street" (*Enchantment* 168), as recounted in "Alicia" in *Street of Riches*; Clémence's talk, "full of strange, poetic digressions and weird references to the family dead as though they were living," troubled the young Gabrielle not at all, and the two girls found comfort, Gabrielle as a young child and Clémence as she became more ill, in each other (*Enchantment* 168). Thus, it was Clémence who saw most clearly behind Gabrielle's plans for Europe: "You're leaving us!" — words which, for the rest of her life, Gabrielle heard in her thoughts, haunting her in those times she felt most alone (169).

What happened to this other Roy, as finely tuned and as perceptive as the rest? Mélina alluded to her suspicions only once, during a night in which she and Gabrielle briefly shared a bed in a rooming house prior to Gabrielle's departure for Europe. The following passage is Roy's reconstruction of their revealing conversation:

> "Perhaps Clémence was always prone to mental ill-
> ness," [Mélina] said, "but something awful must have
> happened to bring it on so suddenly. The doctor thought
> at first there'd been some kind of religious trauma. We
> never knew for sure. Clémence wouldn't ever say a word
> to give us any idea what might have happened — and
> that says a lot in itself. But words I heard her say when
> she had bad dreams, and the look in her eyes sometimes,
> and the peculiar way she'd refuse to do certain things,
> made me suspicious that perhaps . . . one day . . . at

confession. . . . She was such a pious little girl, so conscientious . . . she was only fourteen then . . . maybe . . . you know. . . ."

. . . .

"How could you go on praying . . . and believing . . . after having an idea like that!" I scolded. "Turn against the truth of the Church, just because of one priest . . . one poor, tortured creature, for goodness' sake?" she retorted. (*Enchantment* 186)

How could the world that so recently had contained so much beauty for Gabrielle, freshly returned from the paradise of the Little Water Hen, embrace at the same time the tragedy Clémence may have undergone? Roy never tried to answer such a question in her writings, insisting instead "that every sorrow brings enlightenment and each enlightenment reveals more suffering" (*Enchantment* 185). Nonetheless, the incident certainly damaged Gabrielle's opinion of the Catholic Church, an institution with which she never reconciled herself completely, although Bernadette and Vatican II helped heal many wounds.

After Anna's death, Bernadette managed to have Clémence admitted to a government home for the aged who were still ambulatory in Sainte-Anne-des-Chênes, about fifty miles from her convent in Winnipeg. With the help of her "sisters" and the beginning of the relaxation of convent rules, Bernadette managed to visit Clémence fairly often. After a while, however, Clémence began to feel lonely. Enter Adèle. On 5 May 1964, Gabrielle sent a letter Clémence had written her to Bernadette: the letter announced Clémence's intention to leave Sainte-Anne to go live with Adèle in Saint-Boniface. By January 1965, Gabrielle refers to this plan as Adèle's "fantasy" (*Letters* 71). That summer both Bernadette and Clémence visited Gabrielle at her summer home north of Quebec City in Petite-Rivière-Saint-François, a time that inspired much of *Enchanted Summer*, though neither sister actually figures in the narrative. On the way to Gabrielle's home, Bernadette and

Clémence had hoped to stop to visit Adèle, then living near Montreal, but she begged off, blaming her distance from Montreal (short as it was) as making the encounter too difficult. After the pleasant visit to Petite-Rivière, Clémence kept in frequent touch with Gabrielle by letter; by the end of 1965, Gabrielle had convinced herself that despite Adèle's ongoing project to have Clémence for a housemate, Clémence found Adèle too troubling ever to contemplate moving in with her.

In May 1966, however, much to Gabrielle's chagrin, Adèle and Clémence moved in together. The news upset Bernadette so much that, for the first time in her life, she telephoned Gabrielle long distance. Neither sister had any legal authority over Clémence; Bernadette's concern was that, after all the trouble it took her to get Clémence into Sainte-Anne's, Clémence would not be allowed to return there once she left for Adèle's household. Gabrielle's reaction, in a letter to the obviously upset Bernadette dated May 25, is curious, to say the least. After briefly wishing she had news from Bernadette about the two older sisters, Gabrielle offers money to help them get settled. In the next paragraph, she worries over the tax exemption she usually claims for Clémence, then concludes with a wish that all go well and a complaint about her own fatigue. Callous? Maybe. Weary? Definitely. At her wit's end? Probably. The heretofore separate pictures of Gabrielle's brothers and sisters begin to join together to show a taxing impediment to her self-actualization as a writer. Her limited strength, her need for tranquillity, and her marriage kept her in Quebec; the upheavals in the lives of her family reaffirmed the rightness of her decision in 1939, at least in terms of her career, to go no farther west than Montreal.

Of course, the sisters' living together lasted only a short time. If the consequences were not so sad, we would find the brief story of Adèle and Clémence's joint venture rather comic, destined as they were to drive each other crazy. Adèle was a night owl and Clémence an early bird, which meant that, more often than not, one woke up just as the other went to bed. The end of the day brought Adèle to life; drinking strong coffee, she would roam around, coming and going for hours, ruminating over her life, writing her memoirs, generally disturbing her sister. The next morning, Clémence took her turn, looking for distraction in a too quiet house, while Adèle was worn out from her previous night's activities. At the same time, Adèle left Clémence too much to her own disturbed devices; believing that the family tended to overprotect Clémence, Adèle could then rationalize her own sleeping in as "good" for her sister's mental health. Despite Clémence's ability to cope somewhat on her own, as, for example, when her mother broke her hip in the late 1930s (almost preventing Gabrielle's departure for Europe), she was now older, and too many decisions frazzled her. Adèle and Clémence stuck together as long as they could, pitiably preferring the other's company to loneliness, until Bernadette telephoned Gabrielle to announce that she had hospitalized Clémence. A psychiatrist had strongly recommended that Clémence be institutionalized once again. Since, as Bernadette had feared, she could not return to Sainte-Anne, Bernadette had resourcefully found a home run by the Sisters of Providence in Otterburne, southeast of Winnipeg. Gabrielle condemned Adèle for the havoc she played on Clémence's life and gratefully relied, once again, on Bernadette to fix everything, rationalizing that if she, Gabrielle, flew out to Manitoba to help, she would only get in the way.

Clémence always lay heavily on Gabrielle's conscience, partly through guilt, partly through concern, and probably through frustration because nothing could be done for her. As Roy wrote about the fictional Alicia in Street of Riches, "I must tell the story of Alicia; certainly it left the greatest mark upon my life; but how dearly it costs me!" (135). Gabrielle knew, just as she did about her own mother, that she had to keep a physical distance between herself and the concerns of her family or be swallowed by them. While the distance solved her biggest problem, finding "space" for her profession, it never substantially relieved the guilt that plagued her throughout her life and that she never fully resolved. In frustration over Clémence, Gabrielle directed her anger toward cousins and family friends who did not take the time to visit Clémence in obscure little Otterburne. "They treated her as if she were already buried," she laments (*Enchantment* 142). As was typical with Gabrielle, she eventually targeted herself:

> But had I done better, always so busy writing my stories, as though this were my most essential duty? How do you know which duty is the most essential? Perhaps each has its turn and you have to keep hurling yourself this way and that, trying to do justice to one at a time, while the rest are screaming all around you for attention. (*Enchantment* 142)

No one has found an answer to such questions that plague us all, particularly in the 1990s when our most precious commodity, accurately predicted by *Time* magazine a decade ago, is time.

At one point in her autobiography, Gabrielle describes Clémence's existence as "pointless" (133). Perhaps not surprisingly, the tragic character based partially on Clémence in the story "Alicia" dies at a young age, although as the narrator implies, she had passed away much earlier: "*They* buried her, as one buries everybody, whether a person has died on the day of his death — or long before, because, maybe, of life itself" (*Street* 146). Death, in some instances, kindly removes worrisome people from our lives; our guilt and remorse may remain forever quite keen, but at least these people make no more demands. In a passage from her autobiography that echoes the sentiments in the previous quotation, Gabrielle berates herself for not devoting more time to her family:

> My books have taken a lot of time that I might have given to friendship, love — to obligations of the heart. But friendship, love, personal obligations have also taken a lot of time that I might have given to my books.

The result is that neither my books nor my life is well pleased with me these days. (135–36)

While she required solitude for creation, Roy often and consequently felt lonely. Envious of Margaret Laurence's gregariousness, she asks David Cobb, "I wonder why it is . . . that the more honors that come to my door — unsolicited, I should say — the fewer friends I have?" (14). Roy goes on to speculate that unlike her, Laurence probably put friends first before writing. In other words, Roy suffered from no illusions about the sacrifices her choices demanded. Gabrielle Roy worked out for herself a way of life best suited to favour writing and not people. Her decision to force her own hand by staying in Montreal obviously was the first step. A hugely successful first novel added the necessary ingredient of economic independence. Thus, Gabrielle, by giving expression to her own talent, "bought" herself the freedom to live as she chose for the second half of her life, under constraints to no one but herself, although no other taskmaster could have been more exigent. In addition, to assuage some of her guilt, she had at least one sister she could lean on, one family member sensitive to and understanding of the demands Gabrielle's profession made of her, one willing to accept the hurts and disappointments that resulted from being Gabrielle Roy's sister, one who, even if she had not turned to religion, exemplified in daily life the Christian principles of love, charity, and forgiveness: that sister was Bernadette.

LETTERS TO BERNADETTE

Thanks to an edition of letters written by Gabrielle to Bernadette from 1943 until Bernadette's death in 1970, assembled and edited by Gabrielle's friend, critic, and executor of her literary estate, François Ricard, one can learn much about Gabrielle's daily life and her interactions with her family, and witness the subtle but growing rapprochement between the two sisters. In these letters, the youngest of the five sisters depends heavily on the next eldest to manage family affairs until, when Bernadette falls gravely ill from inoperable renal cancer, the roles reverse and Gabrielle, like Father Perfect, seeks to ease her beloved sister's passage into the next world.

Gabrielle loved Bernadette for her passion, her exuberance, her spontaneity, her love for nature, her meditative religious fervour, her silent suffering for the world around her. Gabrielle remembered the distinctive sound of her footsteps, how on her visits home she would pick up the young Gabrielle and spin her around in a warm hug, veil and voluminous skirts askew. In "A Bit of Yellow Ribbon," Roy pays homage to her sister, the beautiful, twenty-year-old Dédette, who loves driving in automobiles and wearing beautiful clothing and who decides to become a nun. In the story, the young narrator, enchanted by her older sister's room, full of wonderful clothes and accessories but off limits to her, espies one day a bit of yellow ribbon hanging out of a drawer. This ribbon, coveted beyond everything else by the child Christine, helps her accept happily the sister's decision to enter the convent, for she will renounce the secular world and its worldly possessions, including that bit of ribbon the girl hopes to inherit. Juxtaposed with the family's brave but anguished acceptance of Dédette's decision — the mother laments to the young narrator, "She will give up, before her time, her share of the world, her youth, even her freedom!" — the child's self-absorbed quest and innocent vanity form a delightful, even comic, counterplot (*Street* 55).

Of all the Roy children, Bernadette seemed to have loved life the most and therefore had the most to give up. Her decision to renounce the world — made initially at the age of eleven when she had awakened one day, probably at her Uncle Excide's lovely home, to the smells of breakfast mixed with the fragrances of flowers and a new day on earth — resulted from her overwhelming gratitude to God for the beauty and loveliness of his creation. Trained as a teacher, Bernadette did work as a lay instructor until she became a nun in 1919 at twenty-three years of age, entering the convent of the Holy

Names of Jesus and Mary. She completed her novitiate in Montreal, where she took her vows and assumed the name Sister Léon-de-la-Croix. She returned west in 1921 and spent over two decades doing missionary duty in Kenora and in Keewatin in northwest Ontario, not far from the Manitoba border. As a teacher, Bernadette specialized in diction and dramatic arts, even writing and staging a few plays. The convent at Kenora was poor; the one at Keewatin was even more financially distressed, but there she was Mother Superior at a school for young girls. Of all her religious life, Bernadette spent her happiest times there. She eventually returned to Saint-Boniface, where she taught until she retired in 1966 at the Académie Saint-Joseph, the same school Gabrielle had attended as a youngster.

Bernadette's life was as vibrant with emotion, passion, and sensitivity as that of her siblings; her greatest expression of her love for the world lay in her renunciation thereof, dedicating her life to the creator of the beauty she so admired in nature and devoting herself to a life in service of other people. Both Bernadette and Gabrielle realized that any possibility for happiness in their own lives meant independence from their family. While the two women pursued very different avenues in fulfilling their greatest desires, they shared similar qualities of openness, vivacity, and sense of purpose that saved them from the stifling confines of the Roy family, although the two were always ready to lend a helping hand when the call came. Bernadette was the only one in the entire family and among only a handful in general who encouraged Gabrielle to leave for Europe. As Gabrielle observed, the closed French Catholic community which had raised her to a life of sacrifice, self-denial, and discipline lacked sympathy for one who abandoned its cause or refused to assume her already defined position. On the other hand, the most Catholic of them all, Bernadette, took the time to listen to Gabrielle's distress call and to look her squarely in the face, to empathize with the worry and the confusion there, to understand her little sister's anguish; perhaps it echoed her own — in short, Bernadette took the troubled woman in her arms and "in whispers as impassioned as if she were putting her eternal salvation at stake, she told [her]: 'Go! Go! Go!' " (*Enchantment* 171). From that moment on and especially once her sister's success as an author became definite, Bernadette did all in her power to free Gabrielle from family responsibilities. Even at the time of her death, Bernadette took special care to relieve her sister of the burden of caring for Clémence, handing her over into the care of a Sister Berthe and thus leaving Gabrielle at peace to continue her writing.

Roy experienced the essence of Bernadette's spirit during a visit by her sister to Gabrielle's summer cottage, an experience that inspired her *Enchanted Summer*:

> [It is] a strange book, I'll admit, which has an appearance of humour but underneath is deeply serious. Whatever its failings, I think it does capture the essence of Dédette, her open, childlike spirit, her lifetime of yearning so determinedly repressed. (*Enchantment* 173)

Enchanted Summer, a beautiful collection of stories, celebrates the area and the people around Gabrielle's summer home in Petite-Rivière-Saint-François. If nature never failed to move Gabrielle, the same held true for Bernadette. When she went on her annual vacation to a camp by Lake Winnipeg owned by her religious community, Bernadette's subsequent letters to her sister in Quebec brimmed with the spells nature had cast on her during those short periods away from convent responsibilities. If Roy's tender, evocative, amorous descriptions of the natural world in *Enchanted Summer* echo similar descriptions in her other stories, what distinguishes these stories is the perception of the humble and beautiful not as entities unto themselves but as instances of God's universe. If anyone could lead the disillusioned Roy back to a religion that repelled her with its punishing glare which sought out only the sinful and ugly, Bernadette could; and so she did. Then came Gabrielle's turn to reciprocate: in the last days of

Bernadette's life, she wrote daily to her sister, loving letters in which she reminded the ailing nun not only of the joy that lay ahead of her in the next world but also of how her presence had graced this world. Of all the brothers and sisters, who in their own way affected Gabrielle's life and work, she must have felt truly indebted only to Bernadette; the others took, giving little in return. Bernadette only gave, freeing Gabrielle to do what she did best — writing.

TEACHING AND ACTING

Roy finishes her lengthy autobiography by portraying herself in her miserable room on Stanley Street in Montreal after her return from Europe, amazed at the insipid sentences generated by her typewriter. At this particular moment in her development, she had yet to plumb deeply enough within herself to find the literary subjects in all their sorrow and joy that would enchant readers worldwide. Her final sentence — "Yet a bird, almost the minute it's hatched, I'm told, already knows its song" (*Enchantment* 410) — sums up all the dynamism, for good or for ill, of the human condition; it's the *not* knowing that distinguishes us from all other creatures, leaving us with the terrible responsibility to make our own choices. After graduating from normal school, Gabrielle gave Manitoba and Mélina her best shot for eight more years until $800, scrimped and saved over those years, offered her the opportunity to confront the person she feared the most: herself.

If Roy's portrayal of the teacher in *Children of My Heart* reflects even only in part Gabrielle Roy the teacher in the 1930s, students must have loved her, and she must have made a lasting impression on at least a few of them. Roy was lucky, too, both in normal school and in her jobs; her luck in landing a position in the first place and eventually one close to home in the second place must be among the reasons people were driven to despair when she gave it all up to "find herself."

Barely out of teachers college, Gabrielle found herself with a job right away for the month of June in a French school in the French village of Marchand, about fifty miles southeast from Saint-Boniface. Gabrielle was ecstatic, while her mother considered the place the boondocks. Her mother's reaction clearly prefigured her future responses to anything that took her daughter away. One can only imagine her complacency when Gabrielle landed a position in Saint-Boniface a year later, mistakenly thinking that here finally was a daughter and an income on which she could always count. In the meantime, Roy finished her month at Marchand and then found herself three months later in Cardinal, this time southwest of Winnipeg but proximate to Uncle Excide's home and to her lively cousins. It was during this academic year that she almost killed herself trying to traverse marshy, mired terrain to reach her only reminder that life had some pizzazz to it. Cardinal, a little bigger and a bit more prosperous than Marchand, held about as much interest for Gabrielle as a rusty nail. Nonetheless, Marchand and Cardinal were not without their place in Roy's life, since each served as inspiration for a story, "The Dead Girl" in *Enchanted Summer* and "To Earn My Living . . ." in *Street of Riches*. Roy felt that her year at Cardinal, empty as it was in some ways, turned her from a spoiled child into a hardworking, first-rate teacher, good enough at least to get posted at the Académie Provencher in Saint-Boniface the following year, just down the street from rue Deschambault. Although she left the teaching profession for good in 1937, Roy always professed that she loved teaching, working with children, the learning experience. Teaching, however, would have precluded writing. Yet a line from the conclusion of "To Earn My Living . . ." expresses not how she felt in retrospect about her time in Cardinal but rather the happiness teaching brought her: "I did not fully realize it yet — often our joys are slow in coming home to us — but I was living through one of the rarest happinesses of my life" (*Street* 246). If she had despised teaching, the decision to leave her job in 1937 would have been much easier, to be sure. In 1975, when officials from Toronto named a new French-speaking school after her — the École Publique Gabrielle Roy — she appreciated the gesture greatly, taking as much pride in having her name on a school as she did from seeing it on a book's cover.

The Académie Provencher, a public school which combined elementary and secondary levels and attracted about one thousand students, all boys, was located opposite the girls' school Gabrielle had attended. She owed her job to the Académie Provencher's principal, Brother Joseph Hinks, who, while ostensibly focused on his rose garden, kept his eye on the young girls walking to school from across the street, judging their individual characters should any of them apply in the future to teach at his school. As should no longer surprise us in our growing understanding of Gabrielle as a gifted and charismatic individual, Brother Joseph had long favoured the intense young woman who excelled in her high school studies. And he assigned her, once she was on his staff, not the first-grade class of French-speaking children as might be expected, but the other beginning class comprised of non-French-speaking children. Not that these children were Anglophones by any means. Indeed, in this particular situation her father's influence in her life played an instrumental role, for he had taught Gabrielle a sensitivity to the plight of immigrants. Here Gabrielle faced young charges of any origin except that of French or English: Russian, Polish, Italian, Spanish, Czech, Dutch, et cetera. Thanks to her father's job and his generous attitudes toward others, Roy's writings are marked by an empathy for others, and not just for immigrants but for the poor, disenfranchised, old, infirm, defeated, and misunderstood everywhere, from a tormented bank teller to a single Eskimo mother. Roy characterizes herself as born to serve the League of Nations and, aside from her father's own dreams, credits the immigrant children as having fostered and enhanced the hope she always carried within her of universal understanding. Suffice it to say, in her classroom Roy endeavoured to ensure that students never felt that they were either strangers or foreigners.

For a period of time during her years as a teacher (1929–37), Roy joined with a band of young people from Saint-Boniface to form a sort of travelling variety show. Depending on their respective talents, the members sang, danced, played music, clowned, or, as in Roy's case, delivered monologues. They were a group of perhaps a dozen talented, energetic, Francophone, and dedicated individuals — their "gate receipts," such as they were, went to the Jesuit College of Saint-Boniface, usually on the brink of financial disaster, in common with other private institutions of its kind. Their audiences were the inhabitants of the isolated, French-speaking parishes of Saint-Boniface. In the days before television, departments of cultural affairs, and national endowments, this troupe of enthusiastic amateurs must have brought great pleasures to the various rural areas they visited, its spontaneous exuberance as welcome as its performances. The pianist was good, able to stir up his listeners with the boogie-woogie or to soothe them with a gentle waltz. Of particular note was the cartoonist. He would set up his easel on a stage and begin to draw someone he had silently picked from that audience; the murmur would slowly crescendo to a roar as the audience came to recognize the person being drawn.

Given Roy's delicate health as a child and her continual battles with her health after she became a writer, her energy during these years is surprising. She and her friends, after a hard day's work — Roy herself facing between forty and fifty children between the ages of five and six — would pack up their two battered cars with all their stage props and drive off into the sunset, heading for some unknown parish to perform in barns, warehouses, schoolrooms, wherever these small islets of people could provide space. At times, they performed by actual gaslight. Once returned home, bouncing off the walls from the excitement of the evening, Gabrielle would awaken her mother and reenact the evening's highlights.

Critics and Gabrielle Roy herself often commented on Mélina Roy's capacity for storytelling, although it would be unfair to omit her father's stories of "his" immigrants that marked his daughter emotionally and were not without their influence in fine-tuning her talents. If Léon, whom Mélina's embellishing of facts often frustrated, taught his daughter to hold truth in high regard, her mother's wonderful stories nevertheless "taught her to prefer fiction to fact" (Hind-Smith 73–74). Mélina, Roy describes as "Scheherazade," a woman who, despite her family and financial woes, could turn any event into a good yarn, a woman whose fantasies where everyone lived happily ever after probably provided a needed although temporary hiatus from the grinding realities of daily life. If anything could assuage Gabrielle's guilt over her mother, knowing that she had made her laugh did the trick, for remembering those moments assured her that she was more than just a cause for sorrow in Mélina's life. And so Gabrielle's talents at mimicking others — sometimes she could be quite wicked in her parodies — and telling diverting snippets from an evening's outing delighted her mother, who was as good a listener as she was a storyteller. From these rehashings, Gabrielle also learned an important lesson as a writer: a story will not wait. If a story is ready but the writer is not, the writer will lose that story. At the same time, a writer cannot hurry along a story; the story, on its own, will develop and mature as it sees fit. Furthermore, once a story is brought to life, overworking it, constantly making more adjustments, can drain a narrative of its vitality, causing it to flop as flat as a poorly timed joke. In exasperation once, when Mélina asked Gabrielle to tell one story for the umpteenth time, the daughter complained that nothing remained of the story, repetition having stripped the tale of its vigour and spontaneity. Mélina's retort — that one must find a new way to tell an old story, or combine it with other stories, or simply make up a new story — anticipates her daughter's craft. Roy is well known for the autobiographical references in much of her oeuvre, but taking literally these experiential details misses the point and limits recognition of Roy's artistic achievements. Although Roy exploits her own experiences in her stories, her art lies not in rendering the facts but in creatively adding, omitting, and recombining them with a large dose of inventiveness to universalize the events. Life is not art.

As we have seen, Roy possessed all along an author's requisite talents, which, although vaguely leading her toward the vocation of a writer, for many years found expression in the theatre. Her more disciplined incursion into this area while still a teacher in Saint-Boniface was with Le Cercle Molière, a serious theatrical troupe under the direction of Arthur Boutal. Boutal and his wife Pauline, who assisted with Le Cercle Molière, were both instrumental in Saint-Boniface in the preservation of the French language, tastes, and culture. Thanks to Brother Joseph Hinks, who seems to have blessed Gabrielle in many ways during her years at the Académie Provencher, the group received permission to use Roy's classroom to practise its productions. Breathing the chalk dust, which would account in part for the demise of her theatrical ambitions, Gabrielle blossomed during these rehearsals, which allowed her to traverse the boundaries that circumscribed her life as a spinster teacher and to experience other life-styles and destinies, usually more enticing than her own. The play that probably appealed to her the most treated the life of La Vérendrye, the Canadian explorer (1685–1749) born in Trois-Rivières, Quebec, whose adventures took him west, always in the quest for new horizons, where he became a folklore hero to the French Canadians.

A motley crew if ever there was one — teachers, doctors, butchers, shoemakers — these "actors" came together under the inspired direction of Arthur Boutal, himself a printer, and his wife, Pauline, who illustrated fashion catalogues. The Boutals' good taste, refined manners, and fervent dedication to the French way of life brooked no mediocre interpretation on the part of their theatre group. Le Cercle Molière, definitely less obscure than Gabrielle's travelling variety show gang, offered their productions in a proper theatre before audiences that could number a thousand people, including, at times, the governor himself. The troupe even travelled to Ottawa for the annual Dominion Drama Festival, all expenses paid. There, during an intermission one time, the then prime minister, Mackenzie King, trod on the train of Gabrielle's beautiful pink costume, winning her an awkward, timid smile. In an article for a collection on the theatrical and musical history of Saint-Boniface, Roy mentions, somewhat wryly, that the contestants from Quebec were the only ones during this festival to treat the Manitoba group with some disdain ("Chapeau bas" 122). Gabrielle's previous experiences in Quebec, when she travelled there one summer with friends, armed her for the Québécois loftiness. During that earlier trip, the political distance between the Québécois and their brothers and sisters in the other provinces surprised her; welcomed not as a lost relative returned to the fold, as she saw herself, she was regarded instead as a curiosity from the West who spoke French. Given these less than auspicious first contacts, Gabrielle nevertheless, in 1939, settled in Quebec permanently, although her first impressions had caused her to erase this future home from her list of potential destinations in 1937. Regardless of the attitude of the Québécois during the drama festival, Roy was quick to acknowledge the warmth shown to her by Marcelle Barthe, then in her early years of directing, and by Guy Beaune, who later became director of the Grand Théâtre de Québec ("Chapeau bas" 122). Happily, during the years Gabrielle studied as an actor with Le Cercle Molière her troupe twice won the Bessborough Trophy, the national prize for the best interpretation in the French language. One Winnipeg review of the period compliments Gabrielle for her intelligent acting, her diligence, and, of course, her sensitivity; thus, her forays into drama being not without their own success, we can understand that Gabrielle's decision to pursue the study of theatre overseas was not without foundation. And, in the history of Canadian culture and of Francophonie, efforts of such dedicated people as Gabrielle helped fuel the now millions of dollars granted to support colloquia, international travel, and research into a culture that remains vitally alive and well today.

In retrospect, interpreting the lives of others only furthered Roy in her pursuit of a career. Although she would continue to bang her head against the closed door of the theatre in Paris and in London, from expressing the words of another author evolved the desire to give voice herself to personages of her own creation, realizing as she eventually did that her talent lay more in imagining characters than in interpreting them. Her particular forte was giving voice to the silent, to those too long without a literary presence.

Thus Gabrielle spent her twenties during the 1930s, teaching by day and acting by night with her travelling show or under the direction of the Boutals. During her one year at Cardinal, Roy earned a monthly salary of $110, but because of the Depression her salary was reduced to $96. During her tenure at the Académie Provencher, she lived at home with her mother and Clémence. Eventually, they became upstairs borders in their own home when her mother finally sold it. As mentioned previously, Gabrielle saved around $800 during her eight years of teaching, augmenting the sum to $900 by selling a few personal belongings. Her passport applied for and her passage already booked, despite family and community opposition, Roy had only to await her departure date to embark, laden with misgivings but driven by something she could not define. Then her mother broke her hip.

Mélina arrived back from Uncle Excide's, her arms full of her kitchen exploits of jams, jelly, butter, and fresh cream, late in October 1936, late enough that the frost had already made its presence felt and the first snows were imminent. Although overtired and thinner from a summer of exertions at her brother's, and despite Gabrielle's opposition and anger, Mélina determinedly set out the next day for her sister's home in Winnipeg to share some of her bounty from Excide's farm. Mélina's stubbornness was not entirely unknown to her daughter, who had often scolded her for pushing herself too hard, for overtaxing her strength. Mélina no more listened to her daughter than the daughter had listened to her mother on previous occasions. On her way to her sister's house, Mélina slipped on ice and broke her hip — an injury that not only affected Mélina but also threatened to undermine all Gabrielle's plans for Europe. Her mother's hospitalization and surgery, recounted in detail in Roy's autobiography, form another one of those magic episodes in Gabrielle's life where, despite insurmountable obstacles, a fairy godperson appears to unclutter the way. That fairy, here in the guise of Dr. Mackinnon, eventually got Mélina back on her feet after some doubt about whether she would ever walk again, and through his actions he also got Gabrielle to Europe. Recognizing that Gabrielle and her mother were not rich, the good doctor immediately reduced the fee from $250 to $100. Probably in despair and in shock, Gabrielle all of a sudden poured out her ambition, in all its confusion, uncertainty, and indecisiveness, to travel to Europe, insisting that she had to leave soon or what little courage she had to draw on would probably desert her. In his answer, Dr. Mackinnon echoed Bernadette: "Go! Go before life swallows you the way it's swallowed so many of your people." (*Enchantment* 158). He then freed Gabrielle, as we noted earlier, by allowing her to repay him in the future, her conscience determining the amount.

To earn those final few extra dollars to support herself abroad, Roy took a job in the summer of 1937 in the hinterlands of Manitoba three hundred miles north of Winnipeg, a job that became one of the main inspirations for *Where Nests the Water Hen*. The Little Water Hen had one of the few schools kept open during the summer months by the Manitoba Department of Education; because of the area's remoteness and harsh climate, schools such as this one conversely closed for the winter. Gabrielle wanted the job; the local people would provide her room and board, and the geographical location ensured that she would pocket her salary of five dollars a day. In a white linen suit, totally unsuitable for the unexpected, crazy trip she would take just to arrive at her destination, Roy boarded the train in Winnipeg, little suspecting the lasting enchantment the Little Water Hen would hold for her. For these few months meant a visit to one of the most wonderful places on earth, a renewal of her belief in the possibilities for humankind, and a book that became a popular choice in school curricula throughout Canada and elsewhere.

After riding an overnight train to Dauphin, Gabrielle had to remain at the station, since the connecting train to Rorketon was unpredictable and could arrive within minutes or hours. Exhausted and rumpled, she looked rather worse for wear. The stationmaster, taking pity on her, invited Roy to rest in his own bed, his wife being away on holiday and having left the bed with fresh sheets. Awkward as the situation was, Gabrielle chalked this man up under the category Good Samaritan instead of Evil Incarnate, and all to her benefit. Eight hours later, she awoke refreshed and ready for further adventure. Transformed into one of Roy's characters, this stationmaster would later inspire Luzina's confidence "that you need only place yourself under another human being's protection for him to behave towards you as you would wish" (*Enchantment* 176).

The trip to Rorketon brought new fellowship. Other than Roy, the train carried a Department of Health nurse, a businessman who was all reports and papers, and a cattle dealer who came to life later as Isaac Boussorvsky in *Where Nests the Water Hen*. A brakeman generously shared his pot of stew with the passengers, and the engineer stopped the train for ten minutes so Roy could pick a bouquet of flowers. After spending the night at Mrs. O'Rorke's boarding-house in Rorketon, Roy joined the post office inspector, Mr. Jos Vermander, and a Métis guide for the final leg of the trip in a battered Ford. Roy's spirits fell when they entered Portage-des-Près, comprised of a few wooden houses, a chapel, and the semblance of a school. But her actual destination lay another thirty miles beyond, on an island surrounded by two rivers. Vermander kindly shepherded her these last miles.

Once arrived on the island, Gabrielle organized her life to keep boredom at bay. She would awaken early to write, a routine she continued throughout her stay even though nothing she wrote brought her the least satisfaction. Her students, seven in all — four from the house and three who would arrive by boat from other areas — learned reading, writing, and arithmetic, and something about their French heritage. She made an effort to do some lessons in English, but since such conscientiousness on her part to adhere to the dictates of the Department of Education would make little difference in the lives of her French-speaking charges, Roy allowed herself some compromise. The intensity of the midafternoon sun drove them all from the schoolhouse to swim in the pristine waters of the Big Water Hen. In the evenings, Roy and Mme Côté, the mother of the four children in the house in which Gabrielle boarded, walked along various rough paths, followed in single file by "four hens, three cats, the dog, a piglet, the rooster, and, inevitably, a good number of the lambs and ewes that roamed free on the island" (*Enchantment* 181).

Rather than inspiring a sense of drudgery or of oppression, the Little Water Hen experience proved an important hiatus in Roy's life, one of the three or four she experienced that brought her both physical and emotional renewal and kept the frailty of her health from overwhelming her. At the Côtés' that summer, Roy lived in a bubble, forgetting the past and unmindful of the future. What she did not know then and would not begin to realize until 1947 was that she left the Little Water Hen with a book intact, yet to be born, yet to be coloured by the ten intervening years, but nevertheless nascent in the far corners of her mind, waiting for her to find its author, who also lay dormant within her.

THE PATH TAKEN

Before the novelist came the reporter. Those who have experienced the pleasure of reading Gabrielle Roy's work as a freelance reporter, most of it written between the years 1939 and 1945, appreciate the vivid portrayals of places and people, the accompanying intelligent and evocative interpretations, and definitely Roy's engaging style and writing excellence. Discussing the role that her years as a reporter played in her becoming a literary artist, Roy told Myrna Delson-Karan that the journalistic experience helped her a great deal, teaching her especially to respect accuracy (198). But because these numerous articles appeared in journals that today can be found only in archives, mostly on microfiche or on microfilm, and because Roy wrote almost without exception in French, their audience has remained regrettably limited. Fortunately, a few of her representative articles, resurrected and published first in a French edition entitled *Fragiles lumières de la terre* (1978) and later translated into English by Alan Brown as *The Fragile Lights of Earth* (1982), are now available to help readers appreciate more fully the extent of Gabrielle Roy's considerable talents.

Without fanfare, Roy reached Montreal from war-clouded England in April 1939 (approximately five months prior to Hitler's invasion of Poland, which began World War II), heart-sick and wanting to die, so keenly was she gripped by a sense of failure in everything, including love, drama, and writing. This city of slush did little to lighten her mood. Nor for the most part did her miserable room on Stanley Street, with its window overlooking Montreal's main bus station, a portal that let in not the scent of Epping Forest flowers but the noxious fumes of idling buses. On the other hand, this same bus station and the city of Montreal with their promise of departure and travel attracted Roy, making her feel a bit at home: "the cries of 'On track Number 11 . . . ,' *'Sur le track Numéro Onze . . . ,'* gave her a curious sense of security, the feeling that she could up and go if she wanted" (Cobb 10). Within a few days, moreover, she made her first friend, the employee who looked after checked baggage at Windsor Station, the train depot which was also nearby. Roy felt a certain attachment to her trunk, for it not only contained her scant possessions but also evoked many fond memories. This battered trunk, which had frequently proved such an inconvenience in Europe, again posed a problem — now it was too large to fit in her small room, obliging her to leave the cumbersome object and many of its contents at the station. The baggage attendant, a man named Pat Cossack, highly amused at Roy's comings and goings — exchanging a pair of brown shoes here for a pair of beige there — soon began to refuse her tips. After a month he helped her to find a happier place to live on Dorchester Street in a house adjoining his own, where he often passed a share of his stew from his window to hers. Penniless and friendless as Gabrielle was, Pat Cossack's spontaneous empathy and charity did much to renew her spirits. Cossack eventually found Roy room and board in a house run by a Miss McLean where, in comparison with her first two lodgings, Roy considered herself "in the lap of luxury" (*Enchantment* 406). Once again, thanks to the kindness of strangers, Roy felt her morale boosted and her courage revived, allowing her to forge ahead with a degree of confidence. It seems only fair that the disreputable trunk which had too often been a burden eventually repaid its owner handsomely for all of her frustrations on its behalf!

Living on Dorchester Street proved significant, for her long walks eventually took her through both the affluent Westmount area located above Dorchester and the impoverished suburb of Saint-Henri below. Contrasts between the haves and the have-nots, occurring so frequently in Roy's life and works, colour many of her articles and early short stories. And even more significant, during her walks along the old Lachine Canal in Saint-Henri, she discovered "the people that was my own, and its tragedy, and its sadness, and its gaiety too," all of which provided a foundation for her first novel (Cameron 134).

Thus began a period of time that much later Roy described to Joyce Marshall as " 'glorious years' — her apprenticeship as a writer" (37). But in 1939 success still lay in the future; rather than seeing her present plight as glorious, Roy saw only her desperate need for money. Indeed, she needed to earn her living. However stifling and mundane the concept of "earning a living" strikes the imaginative and idealistic Christine in *Street of Riches* — "How mean, it seemed to me, how selfish, how grasping! Must life be earned?" (238) — harsh reality gave Gabrielle Roy little choice. Although terrified by the idea of depending on writing to make her way, Roy did not, like one of her characters, the young and poverty-stricken Florentine in *The Tin Flute*, opt to become either a waitress in a five-and-dime or a sales clerk in a cheap department store. Instead, she doggedly made the rounds of magazines and weekly newspapers throughout the city of Montreal, even though she had only a handful of writings to illustrate her talent. In addition to the three articles published in 1938–39 in the Parisian journal *Je suis partout*, which brought her such satisfaction while staying with Esther and Father Perfect, Roy had a few credits to her name. *Le samedi* in Montreal, for instance, had published two short stories in May and October 1936, respectively, "La grotte de la mort" and "Cent pour cent d'amour." In December of 1936 the *Toronto Star Weekly* had published "Jean-Baptiste Takes a Wife" (the English translation of "Bonne à marier," which appeared in *La revue moderne* in Montreal in June 1940). In addition, *La liberté et le patriote* in Saint-Boniface included the following articles Gabrielle had written in 1938: "Choses vues en passant . . ." (July), "Si près de Londres . . . si loin . . ." (October), "Londres à Land's End" (October), and "Les jolis coins de Londres" (December). And finally, in December of 1938, Montreal's *Le devoir* published "Une grande personnalité anglaise, Lady Francis Ryder," and Winnipeg's *Northwest Review* accepted "Bruges." None of these articles exceeded more than a column or so in length, and, as the various titles suggest, all the stories belong to the category of "human interest," treating local colour rather than the more serious topics Roy eventually tackled in her nearly fifty articles written for *Le bulletin des agriculteurs* in the 1940s. (For a complete list of Roy's journalistic endeavours, consult the three bibliographies by Marc Gagné, François Ricard, and Paul Socken.) On the other hand, these short pieces already reflect both her tendency toward exactitude in recounting personal experiences as well as her interest in social commentary.

Immediately after her arrival in Montreal, Roy wrote her first articles and stories for *Le jour* and *La revue moderne*, promised three dollars by the former for a short column on a subject of her choice and ten dollars by the latter for a slightly longer piece *if* her writing style suited the journal's readers.

Forced to write for a living, Roy sat bravely in her little room, typewriter on her knees, breathing the bus fumes from the station below her window, and did just that. Published weekly, *Le jour* treated political, literary, and artistic subjects. Between May 1939 and March 1940, Roy contributed, in addition to two short stories, some thirty or more columns, beginning with "Amusante hospitalité" and ending with "L'hospitalité parisienne." The articles, short and generally humorous, either related anecdotes about British and Parisian customs or dealt with aspects of life in Montreal: London teatime, the fate of cats and pigeons in London, travel in the south of France, Montreal landladies, scenic Montreal. Writing mostly in the first person from an amused but appreciative point of view, Roy shared her personal perspective on Europe and Montreal. Details recalled from her long walks in Europe and now in Montreal provided a good deal of material with which to interest her readers.

A bimonthly publication with a large readership, *La revue moderne* published Roy's story "La conversion des O'Connor" in September of 1939. The first short story written during this important phase of her career, "La conversion des O'Connor" became the basis for a comic play she would later write entitled "La femme de Patrick," still unpublished at this writing (see Ricard, *Gabrielle Roy* 40). Of sufficient quality to be named "best story of the year" by that journal's editors, the narrative concerns Lizzie, a mother and a faithful wife, who determines to leave her unappreciative family and change her depressing life: "I've had enough of the O'Connors, of the whole pack. I want my freedom" (our translation). But as Paula Lewis notes, in this as in other early works by Roy in Montreal, tradition and social strictures represent forces not easily overcome: "As a 1939 *québécoise* woman, however, [Lizzie] adds that there is sufficient food left in the kitchen, and she soon returns from her little escapade to her traditional role in a family that still does not respect her but needs her" ("Feminism" 31).

In these first serious attempts at her craft, motifs began to appear that would permeate all of Roy's future artistic efforts.

During the years Roy wrote for *La revue moderne*, chiefly between 1939 and 1941, that journal accepted eleven other short stories from her. Although these narratives were longer than her pieces published in *Le jour*, Roy still maintained in her articles and short stories a humorous or, as in Lizzie's case, an ironic perspective and tone toward her subjects, aiming often only to entertain her readers. According to François Ricard, Roy centres the majority of her material on foreigners; on those occasions that Montreal provides the setting, the plot or focus concerns foreigners' experiences in the city (*Gabrielle Roy* 40). Indeed, only four of her stories focus on Francophone Montreal: "Le monde à l'envers" (October 1939), "Avantage pour" (October 1940), "Six pilules par jour" (July 1941), and "Embobeliné" (October 1941).

These preliminary forays into professional writing represent, more or less, an exploratory period during which Roy generally tended to follow what was in vogue, responding to her readers' tastes, having yet to find a style suitably her own. Yet, as Dorothy Duncan suggests, Roy "was not impatient. She knew that the job of learning how to write is at least as hard as learning any other profession" (51). Despite her own exasperation at the platitudes that initially seemed to infest her typewritten pages, the hard work brought her a good deal of satisfaction. For here finally she received the on-the-job training that proved so valuable for her professional growth. The hard work also paid enough to allow her to remain in Quebec, keeping her from having to return to Saint-Boniface either to beg for her former position at the Académie Provencher or to take some unimaginative civil service position. As noted earlier, Gabrielle Roy never returned to teaching. Roy was a writer, finally, although it took a six-year apprenticeship to refine her art before she produced in 1945 the novel that stunned French-speaking Canada and revolutionized the direction of its literature.

Eventually Roy offered her talents and energy to a Mr. Soulard, then editor in chief of *Le bulletin des agriculteurs*. According to Marc Gagné, Soulard asked Roy if she could write; in response she offered not her work published in Montreal but the three articles published earlier in *Je suis partout* in Paris. As Gagné tersely states the case, "She was hired" (23; our translation). Working for this journal, she immediately began to evolve from an objective reporter into a more subtle interpreter of human events, becoming in the process a serious and very successful journalist. Thus began a five-year association with this journal, during which time Roy saw her salary rise from approximately $15 per article to the rather impressive wartime payment of $250 for each submission.

During the first part of her new career, the quality of her fiction did not see immediate improvement. For example, François Ricard, easily Roy's most knowledgeable critic, relegates her two early short stories for *Le bulletin*, "Les petits pas de Caroline" (October 1940) and "La fuite de Sally" (January 1941), to the status of "exercises" in preparation for *La revue moderne* (*Gabrielle Roy* 42). These early exercises, however, did include "Le joli miracle" (December 1940), a narrative focused on the poverty in Montreal, which becomes a central concern in *The Tin Flute*. But with her first article for the same journal, "La belle aventure de la Gaspésie" (November 1940), Ricard feels that Roy really hits her stride by doing what she herself knew she did best: writing "on subjects involving fact, reality, close observation" (*Enchantment* 410). In ensuing articles, her ability not only to report analytically about the people, regions, and industries that she visited but also to articulate her own sympathetic points of view soon made Gabrielle one of the most regular and popular contributors to *Le bulletin*. And perhaps Roy's own particular delight in the Gaspé Peninsula area contributed to the success of her articles. Indeed, she wrote parts of *The Tin Flute* during subsequent summer visits to the area. In a letter to Bernadette on 15 September 1943, for example, Gabrielle tells how the warmth and simplicity of the people there helped her unwind and relax, and how she shares their mother's passion for the countryside, the open horizons, the smell of the fresh earth (*Letters* 4). That she developed a

FIGURE 14

Gabrielle Roy, during her journalism years, circa 1942, inter-viewing Adélard Godbout, premier of Quebec from 1939 to 1944.

strong attachment to the place and the people there is evident. As she wrote in a later article about that rugged area of Quebec for *Le bulletin* in May 1944, "The Gaspé had no need of words to speak to me: it was there, alive, beneath my eyes" (*Fragile* 100). Given the wartime climate of a large city such as Montreal and the exhaustion that life in crowded cities often induced in Gabrielle, the peacefulness of this coastline must have seemed like heaven.

LE BULLETIN DES AGRICULTEURS

Roy's collaboration with *Le bulletin des agriculteurs* beginning in 1940 marked a five-year period of intense output on her part: twenty-some short stories and tales, and fifty-some articles, most of which appeared in *Le bulletin*. (Articles also appeared in *Le Canada* and *La revue populaire*, both Montreal publications.) In the spring of 1941, Roy also began writing *The Tin Flute*, first intended as a series of major articles about Montreal but which, inspired by her heartfelt identification with the poor of Saint-Henri, eventually became her first and most famous book. Thus, her long walks through this impoverished area of Montreal, begun shortly after her arrival in the city, affected much more than her journalism.

After two short stories and a few articles on such diverse subjects as the Gaspé region, a visit to a modern farm, and farmer/ceramists, beginning in 1941 Roy found a format suitably her own, which she would continue to practise over the next four years. The style is not without recognizable effects in almost all of her published works after *The Tin Flute*: long separate reports, a tapestry loosely linked on a broad range of subjects published over a period of time. Here we find Gabrielle Roy the artist truly in the making, creating a genre of her own which allowed not only an analytical depiction of the world around her but also personal interpretations thereof. These reports for *Le bulletin* evolved into four major series of articles. From June to September of 1941 she published four in-depth articles under the rubric "Tout

FIGURE 15

*Roy in Bonneville, Alberta, in 1942 during
one of her trips west as a freelance reporter.*

Montréal," in which she detailed the struggling but vital city in the process of creating its own distinct identity. Assessing the good and the bad, Roy invested Montreal with her unique sense of hope and of hope for happiness for urban dwellers, many of whom were forced to contend with poor living conditions and chronic unemployment. And, as she explained to Joan Hind-Smith, she began her first novel shortly after these summer articles on Montreal were published: "Suddenly, one day it was all there — characters, theme, meaning — as a huge, hazy mass, yet with a sort of coherence already" (83). Over the next four years, Roy continued with her job as a feature journalist, which paid her enough to allow her time during her summer vacations in Port Daniel in the Gaspé Peninsula to work on her novel.

Roy's second series of articles, seven in all, entitled "Ici l'Abitibi" and published between November 1941 and May 1942, informs readers about the settlement of colonists on Nepawa Island and its environs in the Lake Abitibi region on the border between eastern Ontario and southwestern Quebec. The third group of articles, "Peuples du Canada," for which she is perhaps best known as a journalist, was published between November 1942 and May 1943 and depicts the lives of seven different immigrant groups in the same number of articles: Hutterites, Doukhobors, Mennonites, Jews, Czechs, Ukrainians, and Québécois. The Canadian mosaic in all its diversity comes under Roy's sympathetic scrutiny, but feeling does not prevent her from adopting at times an ironical stance in relationship to these ethnic groups, whose unique qualities her father had taught her to respect, frequent frustrations notwithstanding. Describing her father's interactions with "his" Doukhobors, she opens "Turbulent Seekers after Peace," one of the seven articles of the series, with the following description:

> When I first heard the word "Doukhobor" I remember being filled with a sentiment of mixed terror, curiosity and an admiration that I find hard to admit. My father,

then a settlement agent in the West, had just come home from one of his long, arduous and dangerous trips. He was frowning, his eyes were hollow from lack of sleep, and, as he finally sank into his armchair, he looked the image of exhaustion.

"Be quiet now," our mother said. "Your father's all in. He's just come back from his Doukhobors." (*Fragile* 31)

As François Ricard aptly points out, this tableau of ethnicity anticipates some of the most beautiful pages from *Where Nests the Water Hen* and *Street of Riches* (*Gabrielle Roy* 44). These articles, in revised form, reappear in *The Fragile Lights of Earth*, except for "Peuples du Canada: les gens de chez-nous," a story about the people of Quebec, for which she substituted "The Gaspé Fishermen — A Sail in the Night" (May 1944) from her series "Horizons du Québec." And these articles bear directly on a most important aspect in all of Roy's fiction, especially as they document the author's commitment to relating the truth about actual people. Allison Mitcham offers high praise when characterizing the essays collected in *The Fragile Lights of Earth*, writing, "Roy's 'actual' people, then, those who emerge from her essays, who are the subjects of her reporting, are so much of the same fiber as the characters of her fiction that the more one reads of Gabrielle Roy's work, the more one is hard pressed to differentiate between the people she has encountered in real life and those she has confronted in her imagination" (*Literary Achievement* 34–35). During this same period, Roy reported on the Al-Can highway and wheat harvests in the Canadian west in a series entitled "Regards sur l'Ouest" for *Le Canada* from December 1942 to January of the following year. Subsequently concentrating her full attention on Quebec, Roy conceived of the twelve-part series "Horizons du Québec" (January 1944 to May 1945). Five articles in the collection treat different regions of Quebec that border water, such as Saguenay-Lac-Saint-Jean, the Ile-aux-Coudres, Gaspé, and Petite-Rivière-Saint-François (Gabrielle eventually purchased a house at Petite-Rivière, so much did the location appeal to

FIGURE 16

Roy on a cod-fishing boat off the
Gaspé Peninsula in the early 1940s.

her); four other stories discuss the Eastern Townships between Montreal and the United States; and three articles deal with professions that bespeak so much of the Canadian ethos: market gardeners, lumberjacks, and timber drivers. Roy concludes her career as a journalist for *Le bulletin* with separate exposés on the cotton, gold, and pulp and paper industries.

If the preceding list of titles and subjects suggests that Roy travelled extensively during these years, that conclusion is accurate. Committed to relating factual material, she only reported on what she had personally experienced, supplemented by ample historical research and, when necessary, the use of an acquired technical vocabulary. Obviously, these experiences broadened her perspective while providing a valuable education. And the assignments certainly proved adventuresome. For her first article on the Gaspé region, *Le bulletin* paid all her expenses (the train trip on the CNR, room and board with a widow at Port Daniel for $8.50 a week), and Roy reports that for her efforts she earned $15 (Labonté 92). Over the course of this particular career, she travelled to diverse areas of Canada by boat, train, and car. In addition, Roy accompanied a group of colonists 1,300 miles from the Iles de la Madeleine in the Gulf of St. Lawrence to Lake Abitibi and remained with them as they settled in, an experience that certainly recalled to her the numerous times her own father made similar journeys to found new settlements for immigrant families of diverse ethnic backgrounds and religious denominations. All on her own, she stayed with a group of Hutterites and with a Jewish family from Sudetenland out west, with a fisherman's family in Gaspé, with loggers in a logging camp; she also descended to the bottom of a mine and journeyed down the Assomption River with timber drivers. The twenty-eight-year-old teacher who embarked tentatively on a European adventure in 1937 is practically unrecognizable in the well-travelled, competent, knowledgeable, highly respected journalist of 1945 who seemingly thrived on unpredictable situations and took pleasure in cutting herself off from the outside world.

What happened to the reclusive Gabrielle Roy, shut in a depressing room in London feeding shillings to a heater that provided little heat? Where was the woman so desperate for escape, having already found such seclusion twice, once at the Little Water Hen and once in Epping Forest? Almost as though life had finally given her the go-ahead signal, Roy gathered momentum and was not to be stopped. The adventurer out for a good time in Provence turned into the adventurer who had found her calling. All her endurance, initiative, temerity, capacity for hard work, and intellectual brilliance she now channelled into what she did best: writing. She wrote, moreover, about what interested her most: human relationships. And she wrote using the method that was her forte: close, analytical observation. By all accounts she had a wonderful time honing her talent.

The turning point for Roy, what Ricard labels her "conversion to reality" (*Gabrielle Roy* 43; our translation), began with her articles about Montreal in 1941 as the city prepared to celebrate its tricentennial. Roy abandoned her more whimsical, light-hearted treatment of reality. In her earlier articles about Quebec, she had expressed great pride in the province's potential for industrial growth and argued in favour of embracing modern development, extolling technology's promise of greater freedom for all. Instead, she now plumbed reality's depths, revealing all its seriousness, beauty, and horror. Even more important, introspection assumed a subordinate position in her work, giving way to a more outward-looking appraisal of the complex world around her. Roy is particularly famous for her walks around various neighbourhoods in Montreal during the early 1940s, walks that took her, after two years, into the squalid corners of Saint-Henri. As she soon discovered, the people living in this district of Montreal "were not beneficiaries of industrialism, they were its casualties" (Hind-Smith 82).

Wittingly or unwittingly, Roy possessed a genius for remembering details around her. In reference, for example, to the rather depressing and inward-directed weeks of her initial visit to Paris, Roy wrote:

I tramped through whole districts of Paris feeling that I'd seen and heard absolutely nothing, enclosed in a kind of vacuum that I kept as tightly sealed as I could from the humanity pressing around me. . . .

Years later, however, speech intonations, sounds, smells by the thousand would come back to me from those long walks. I'd see in precise detail a sign at a certain street corner, or the form of a taverner standing in the door of his bistro, beret pulled down over his brow. I had a faculty for storing away details that would be useful to me later. . . . (*Enchantment* 221–22)

Similarly, the memorable scenes from her walks in Saint-Henri would eventually form the substance of *The Tin Flute*. But more significant, with her attention focused outside herself, with the scope of her vision enhanced, she now began to mine her talent of its always rich potential and consequently to depict her own country in what would soon become a shockingly innovative and revolutionary manner of writing.

BIRTH OF A NOVEL

"Tout Montréal," her first series for *Le bulletin des agriculteurs*, served as the genesis for *The Tin Flute*. In this series, as in all of her reporting, Roy concerned herself especially with the ambiance of the locale and its effect on the human condition. Her own childhood in a small, insular city on the prairie, the heritage handed down by relatives (rural emigrants from Quebec who became farmers in Manitoba), and her travels to almost all four corners of Canada combined to make her particularly sensitive both to the movement of peoples from the country to the city and to the influence of technology in both spheres. The family farm, which before could not manage without the help of hired hands, now required merely one person and one tractor — exactly the condition she would encounter later in life during a visit to her Uncle Excide's farm, which his son ran single-handedly with a tractor, returning in his automobile each evening to his "ranch house" in the nearby city. Shocked as she was to find Excide's farmhouse, that seat of so many fond memories, turned into a garage, Roy's broader perspective on reality allowed her to forsake a more limited or elegiac focus on the romantic, mystical notion of the good old days. Besides, she knew all too well how hard work had ground down her forebears.

Coupled with her high hopes for Quebec's future well-being through its accession to the technological era, Roy's acceptance of the inevitability of industrial progress in the country and in the city led her to view the future candidly yet optimistically. Anyone familiar with Roy's novels knows the enchantment land and nature held for her; at the same time, to the uninitiated, fields of wheat whether planted by hand or by machine look identical. Gabrielle Roy preferred neither the country nor the city; she felt comfortable in both, even though she repeated on numerous occasions her belief that modern cities needed to be more "countrified." Roy had the ability to see the pros and cons of industrial progress, to see both sides of the question, and only then to accept facts, and finally to hope for the greater good that could result. Of course, she realized that the degree of "goodness" depended on the movement of humankind toward fraternity and mutual coop- eration; jealousy and competition, she frequently suggested, would only further enslave the working population, a class already divided unto itself. In her despair over the question of divisiveness, Roy focused special attention on the French Canadians, and she contrasted this divisiveness with the spirit of interdependence she discovered in the different ethnic groups that settled as homogeneous entities in western Can- ada. Until her death, Roy insisted that the various groups that make up Canada must unite, adding that if Anglophone and Francophone Canada could manage to "find a way of working together and completing one another, it's quite marvellous what we could do together, quite marvellous" (Cameron 134).

Roy's faith in the future of the country derived from her belief that progress, despite vicissitudes encountered along the way, means betterment of the human condition. For example, in "Après trois cents ans," the last article in the series "Tout Montréal," Roy painted a sylvan picture of the city's birth and decried Montreal's penchant three hundred years later to erect factories and slaughterhouses on some of its most beautiful sites; she nevertheless suggested that the city's grandeur derived from the very forces that threatened to pull it apart. This particular article contains numerous examples of the conflict that pervades Roy's fiction, aptly described by Paula Lewis as "the author's admittedly dual attitude of tragic realism and humanistic idealism" ("Last" 214).

Montreal's quiet birth as Ville-Marie was dedicated to the proposition of saving the souls of its native inhabitants. When commerce arrived in the form of the fur trade, however, the quiet hamlets of the island amalgamated, their geographical location making them ripe for commercial exploitation. Roy evokes, not without some romanticism, the farmers-turned-trappers-adventurers-explorers, the stuff from which legends are created. On the other hand, her story candidly acknowledges that with adventure comes discord, fraud, smuggling, and injustice. And the English. And the Hudson's Bay Company. And a resulting feudal system based on the assumption that some people are more equal than others. As the years went by, and after the capitulation of Quebec City in 1759, the French peasants abandoned their land and customs while the English envisioned Montreal as a vast industrial and cosmopolitan centre. Soon mutual economic interest brought the two languages together: ideally, "Jean-Baptiste" and "John Bull" would flatter each other and compensate for each other's weaknesses. Montreal soon discovered that it was not more French than English, but rather than become a melting pot — an ideal that so delighted Americans during the same period — the society sought to preserve and combine its two dominant elements. Thus, by the twentieth century, Montreal became a city of one million people, constituting one-eleventh of Canada's entire population, which outwardly welcomed peoples from all over the world.

It is French in its exuberance and its political confusion, English in business, cosmopolitan at its ports, American on St. Catherine Street, provincial in the east, puritan in Westmount, snobbish in Outremont, nationalistic at Lafontaine Park, French-Canadian on June 24th, Saxon during Christmas . . . bilingual when necessary and deeply hybrid in its soul. ("Après trois cents ans" 39; our translation)

Roy documented all the weaknesses that resulted from the principal French-English duality, but she acknowledged that Montreal's strength and richness derived from the identical source. Such a duality, in her optimistic and syncretic view, did not mandate a decision to opt for one or the other but instead allowed for choosing the best attributes from both to produce a harmonious balance.

In this city whose contradictions deny and affirm its presence, industrialization created sectors of pollution, filth, and impoverishment. In the early years of World War II, Roy's four articles on Montreal, while envisioning a better future, portrayed a city in full crisis, striving for technological progress but generally oblivious to the bereft human condition left in its wake. And, irony of all ironies, the promise of war galvanized the city, stimulating production and creating what industrialization eliminated: employment. *The Tin Flute* must be understood in the context of this Montreal, a city suffering the vicissitudes that necessarily accompany material progress.

In its infancy, the novel was supposed to be another short story intended for publication in *Le bulletin* or probably *La revue moderne*, Roy's two major sources of income during this period of her life. This short narrative, however, evolved and expanded over three years while Roy continued to earn her living as a journalist. Before being edited into final form, and in a manner typical of so many works that seemingly take on a life of their own, relegating the author's role to that of a mere typist, the manuscript that sat on top of Roy's desk had grown to the unwieldy length of some eight hundred pages by early 1944.

Journalism had opened the way for Roy to capitalize on her powers of observation, sharpen her analytical skills, and create a form and style of her own. *The Tin Flute*, then, was not a novel conceived and developed in organized fashion but the result of Roy's five-year apprenticeship to her craft and to herself. And while *The Tin Flute* derives from Gabrielle Roy's work as a freelance reporter, this novel also marks a conclusion to her days as a journalist. Although she would publish a few more articles and short stories after 1945, all vastly superior to her work of 1939–40, Roy essentially retired from the active public sphere of journalism to a more sedentary and private life-style, dedicating the remainder of her life to writing fiction in relative solitude.

During the summer of 1944, Roy rewrote *The Tin Flute* at Rawdon, a city in the Laurentians north of Montreal in the region where her mother was born. She submitted this manuscript to Gérard Dagenais at Éditions Pascal, a publishing house that appeared during the war and remained in operation only until 1950, but a company that played, nevertheless, an important role in the transformation that Québécois literature was then undergoing. Dagenais wrote later that he read Roy's manuscript in one sitting on a Sunday and that his enthusiasm for this French Canadian novel with its accent on realism made him decide immediately to publish it.

The Tin Flute appeared in Montreal for the first time in two volumes during the summer of 1945. As Dorothy Duncan relates, the French reading public, aside from the denizens of the Saint-Henri slum whose story Roy told, received this first novel with an enthusiasm equal to that of the publisher:

> It was contemporary; it dealt vividly, honestly, and above all without the slightest trace of self-consciousness, with the unfortunate poor in Montreal, who could step out of their misery only when war brought prosperity to the country; it overflowed with good humor,

enormous pity, deep understanding and a fearless will to be truthful. (51)

While the novel deals with the particulars of a specific place and time, the sympathetic rendering of the slum dwellers' plight universalized the treatment of human misery and eventually attracted an enthusiastic and wide-ranging international readership to whom the story speaks even today. In 1946 the young Académie canadienne-française awarded Roy the Médaille "Feu qui dure" for *The Tin Flute*, making her one of the medal's first recipients, and the older Académie française added another prize, the Médaille Richelieu. In 1947 the publisher Beauchemin reissued the novel in two volumes, and the Parisian publisher Flammarion published it in one volume, at the same time contracting with Roy for first refusal of her next five novels. *The Tin Flute* was subsequently translated into English and then into Spanish, Danish, Slovak, Swedish, Norwegian, Romanian, Russian, and at least six other languages. The translation into English established Roy as a major international author. Choosing the novel as its Book of the Month for May of 1947, the Literary Guild of America put into circulation another 750,000 copies of *The Tin Flute*, drawing further attention to the novel, which in turn garnered more awards that same year: the Prix Femina in Paris, making *The Tin Flute* the first Canadian novel to win a major French literary award; the Governor General's Award in Ottawa, the first of three she would eventually earn; and the Lorne Pierce Medal of the Royal Society of Canada, making her the first woman elected a member of the Literary Section of the Royal Society of Canada. In addition, a major Hollywood studio purchased the film rights for the hefty sum of $75,000 and planned to cast Joan Fontaine as the unfortunate five-and-dime waitress, Florentine Lacasse — viewers, however, would not see a film version of the novel until the day of Roy's death, when a Canadian production of the film, directed by Claude Fournier, made its successful debut at the Moscow Film Festival. In 1947 the now wealthy, famous, respected, French

Canadian schoolteacher from the small town of Saint-Boniface had definitely made it.

What had happened? Roy had written a novel and finally found herself in the career she had so long desired and for which she had left a teaching position in Saint-Boniface, sacrificing both financial and professional security. Her long-suffering mother passed away on 26 June 1943, at the age of seventy-six, while Roy was writing *The Tin Flute*; Roy dedicated the book to Mélina Roy. François Ricard, in the biographical essay "La métamorphose d'un écrivain," concludes that Roy's success, deriving as it did from work that kept a roof over her head and food on her table, is based on a misunderstanding, a contradiction (447). By 1947, Roy found herself in the process of writing *The Cashier*, which she did not publish until 1954, while actually giving birth in the meantime to a work radically opposed to *The Tin Flute* and *The Cashier* in theme, setting, and personages: *Where Nests the Water Hen*. The sense of misunderstanding Ricard notes finds affirmation in this complex narrative (neither a novel nor a collection of short stories), Roy's personal favourite, a creation that differed so fundamentally in spirit from the internationally acclaimed *Tin Flute* that Flammarion, although it did publish similar fiction and eventually published Roy's new book, refused to consider *Where Nests the Water Hen* as one of the five novels for which it had contracted. Doubt, uncertainty, isolation, and confusion dogged Roy from 1945 to 1950; she felt that she needed to surpass the success her first novel enjoyed, feeling, as she told Dorothy Duncan, that "My next book must be better than my last" (54). And yet, in retrospect, *The Tin Flute* and *The Cashier* remain atypical instead of typical of her oeuvre. Roy felt torn between a novel that launched the success and recognition she craved and narratives equally her own that drew on the life experiences with which she felt most familiar and actively engaged. In other words, although she felt at home in Quebec and empathy for those whose lives she depicted in her first novel, she could not abandon her Manitoba heritage, which plays such a dominant role in later works such as *Street*

of Riches, The Road Past Altamont, and *Children of My Heart.*
After all the fanfare *The Tin Flute* caused outside of Canada,
however, none of Roy's books ever received another international award. In some respects, therefore, her decision to
write about the Canadian prairies represented a sacrifice of
sorts. But as Roy explained to Donald Cameron, her books
were written as if by command: "I receive an order, and I try
to fill it out. The order is not anything vulgar, or anything
cruel, or anything harsh. It's something quite beautiful and
tender, but it has to be obeyed just the same" (132). And thus
the location of her next novel moved from Montreal, where
she detailed life as it was, to the marshes of northern Manitoba, to the Water Hen district, where she described life as it
could be.

But prior to responding to that inner command to write
Where Nests the Water Hen, Roy had first, in a very real sense,
to overcome her success and the expectations it spawned. The
five-year period between the publication of *The Tin Flute* and
the first of her numerous Manitoba books must be characterized as conflicted:

> I remember when *The Tin Flute* came out in New York,
> there were these cocktail parties and dinners, there
> would be all this fuss, all this attention . . . and then I
> would go back to my hotel room, feeling utterly alone.
> *For years the memory of that success was awful* [our empha-
> sis]. I have, I think, a grateful heart, so what could I do?
> I was paralyzed. It was no longer, Do what you can. It
> was, Do *better.* (qtd. in Cobb 12)

Paris proved no less daunting than New York.

Making it in the French literary world meant, inevitably,
making it in Paris. Arriving there in 1947 with her new husband,
a doctor who would pursue specialized studies in gynaecol-
ogy in Paris and subsequently in Saint-Germain-en-Laye,
about fifteen miles from Paris, until 1950, Roy probably
harboured aspirations of becoming an active member of this

important European city's world-noted literary élite. *The Tin Flute* fit in well with a postwar Paris then caught up in the complex contradictions and societal exigency of existentialism under the tutelage of Sartre, Camus, and Kafka. Existentialism sought a literature of the *engagé(e)* based on societal criticism and portraying the human spirit in all its nakedness before those epistemological questions of being and nothingness, God and Godlessness, the active versus the passive. Such an ambiance demanded from Roy an equivalent of *The Tin Flute*, now expected by her reading public. And so, responding to an order from the outside world, she began a novel that dealt with a middle-class Everyman named Alexandre Chenevert, a character who would eventually become, in her words, "a sounding board for all the communications which bombard us" (qtd. in Hind-Smith 100).

At that time, however, Roy's chronicles of this pitiful man's struggles took the form of two short stories published in 1948 in Paris, "Feuilles mortes" and "La justice en Danaca et ailleurs," and one in Montreal, "Sécurité." In tone, the stories clearly strike a chord of alienation and absurdity. While "Sécurité" may well proceed from the conclusion of *The Tin Flute*, with the suggestion that war, no matter how noble its cause, rends the human spirit, the other two stories not only emphasize existential dread but also clearly echo the themes of *The Cashier*, especially the novel's "atmosphere of imprisonment and absurdity," as Paula Lewis explains:

> Adrien of "La Justice en Danaca et ailleurs" is an insignificant man who works too much. At one point in his life, he works overtime, does not declare the extra income, is audited, and insults the auditor. After his ten-minute revolt, he calmly returns to his role as another *fourmi* of the country. Constantin Simoneau of "Feuilles mortes" is the closest ancestor of Alexandre. He is a solitary, timid man who, without harboring any revolt within him, works too hard, fears losing his job, and accumulates debts. Like Chenevert, he lives with a

constant sense of guilt and paranoia, the feeling that he is being judged. An insignificant man, Constantin is pathetically and poignantly portrayed. ("Feminism" 27–28)

But all three stories possess a less than elegant style, suggesting a less than full commitment on the artist's part. Indeed, Ricard rightly points out in "La métamorphose d'un écrivain" that in these short works Roy abandoned her own inclinations and laboured instead to manufacture the tone, the style, and the seriousness she felt were now expected of her. As a result of this misdirection, Ricard considers Roy's efforts in these narratives constrained, as if she were forcing herself unnaturally into a creative vein that, for her, continually ended in an impasse. In Paris and, in theory, *engagée*, Roy felt herself bound to crown the success of *The Tin Flute* with a similar, better effort, although her next published book took her readers to the pristine waters of the Little Water Hen. She offered Paul Socken this rationalization for temporarily abandoning *The Cashier*: "I couldn't give it a precise setting while I was still in France. It was clear that Alexandre was a Canadian and needed a Canadian setting. So I put it aside and came back to it when I returned to Canada" (*Myth and Morality* 90).

Social realism gave way to a paradise of sorts when Gabrielle Roy, as we described earlier, envisioned her next novel while riding to Chartres in a car with friends. The writing of *Where Nests the Water Hen* began at Epping Forest in 1948 and, according to the last page of the work, concluded in May 1950, in Saint-Germain-en-Laye while Roy and her husband were still in France. Although it would have been wonderful to make a big splash in Paris with a follow-up novel similar to her first, *Where Nests the Water Hen* suited Roy more than *The Tin Flute*, just as Saint-Germain-en-Laye, described by Roy in a letter to Bernadette as "an almost rustic retreat" and "a paradise for meditation," suited her better than Paris (18 Oct. 1948, *Letters* 14–15).

PROFESSIONAL SUCCESS
AND PERSONAL CHANGE

Roy had been out West in 1942 to research her articles on the people of Canada and had to return once again in 1943 for her mother's funeral. Mélina, then, never saw the splendid fruits of her sacrifices for Gabrielle, and the dedication of *The Tin Flute* to Mélina thus strikes a poignant chord. After her mother's death, Gabrielle seems to have turned for emotional and spiritual sustenance to her sister Bernadette, the cloistered nun who was "like the sun," for Bernadette rejoiced at all Gabrielle's successes and was, Roy said, "very very happy over every single good little thing that happened to me" (Cameron 137).

In 1946 Roy wrote to Bernadette that *The Tin Flute*'s success astonished her. Indeed, she often claimed that all the while she was writing the novel, she was surprised that no one else published a book of its kind, for the subject matter struck her as very obvious. She mentioned in the same letter that the English translation would carry a significant monetary reward, going on to describe how the money could be used, not in terms of what she could do for herself, but what she could do for Bernadette and Clémence (4 Jan. 1946, *Letters* 5). In a later letter from France dated 18 October 1948, Gabrielle mentions donating, via her lawyer, Jean-Marie Nadeau, $1,000 to the girls' school where Bernadette taught in Keewatin, Ontario (*Letters* 14). The collected letters to Bernadette contain ubiquitous references to Roy's sending money, at times only five or ten dollars to defray Bernadette's taxi expenses from visiting Clémence.

As these letters attest, Roy's family ties remained strong throughout her life, although she preferred sending money as a substitute for her actual presence. Solitude and peace were indispensable to her work, and her work, as should be clear by now, usually took precedence over everything, including and sometimes especially friends and family. Although Roy claimed to Bernadette that her success and all the subsequent

FIGURE 17

*Roy (left) looking over the shoulder of Donatien Frémont,
manager of Winnipeg's French-language newspaper* La liberté
et le patriote *from 1923 to 1941. Frémont won numerous awards
for his work in support of French culture in western Canada.*

fanfare had left her unchanged (4 Jan. 1946, *Letters* 5), her only way to maintain her self, whom she liked by now, was to shun the limelight. Her essay in *The Fragile Lights of Earth*, "How I Received the Fémina," for example, ostensibly pokes fun at all the political machinations and private manoeuvring behind her nomination for this illustrious literary prize, received in November of 1947. Behind Roy's playful presentation, however, the reader easily detects the author's bewilderment and feelings of deception at finally being named recipient on account of her physical presence in Paris, her gender, and because the Comtesse de Ponge, the president of the Fémina jury, thought it would be a good idea for a Canadian to win the award — on account of anything, that is, except *The Tin Flute*'s considerable merits. Marked for life by the experience, Roy later refused to accept other awards or to accept awards demanding her personal appearance. Twice nominated by her publishers and listed amongst the finalists for the Prix littéraire de la Ville de Montréal in the late 1970s, Roy was disqualified both times because she refused to sign the nomination forms. Reclusive by nature and unable to create when interrupted by the demands her success generated or by daily life in general, Roy retreated from the public sphere for the second half of her life. While she did not exactly become a recluse, Roy aggressively guarded her privacy.

In a way, therefore, Gabrielle Roy's life divides almost in half, into two parts symmetrical in length but opposed in activity. Roy's first thirty-six years, which often found her disoriented and depressed, nevertheless brought into her life travel, the dramatic arts, experience and maturity, and passionate love. She then resigned from her role as active participant in life to devote herself completely to writing. Roy felt that active experience should give way, for a writer, to a time of retrospection and contemplation. Joyce Marshall noted Roy's belief that "writers should seek experience actively in their youth, should travel as much as they could, geographically and emotionally; then at about the age of forty, they could, as she put it, 'draw in'" (41).

FIGURE 18

Newlyweds Dr. Marcel Carbotte and
Gabrielle Roy in Concarneau, France, 1948.

The years between the publication of *The Tin Flute* (1945) and *Where Nests the Water Hen* (1950) were an exciting, stimulating culmination of all that had gone before and set the course for the rest of her life. At the beginning of 1946, Gabrielle wrote to Bernadette from her retreat in the Laurentians describing her difficulties in dealing with all the unwanted publicity; seeing pictures of herself displayed prominently in bookstores and in other public places amazed but distressed her. Roy was unwilling to pay the price of publicity, writing, "At least here in Rawdon my private life is my own, and I like it that way" (4 Jan. 1946, *Letters* 6).

In 1947, Roy travelled out West in the month of May for a breather from all the excitement stirred up by her novel and to look after an ailing Clémence (as always, in need of proper care and supervision) and a recovering Anna. Given her success, Roy's trip to her hometown, the first since her mother died four years earlier, was treated as the return of the prodigal daughter — an enthusiastic account of her presence in Saint-Boniface appeared in Winnipeg's French newspaper, *La liberté et le patriote*. During her stay, Gabrielle received a formal invitation to dinner with Le Cercle Molière — the drama group with whom Gabrielle had travelled and performed years earlier — from its then president, Marcel Carbotte, a young physician also from Saint-Boniface. Although she hesitated to accept, fortunately she did, for that evening she met in Dr. Marcel Carbotte her future husband.

From a feminist perspective, writing Gabrielle Roy's biography comes as something of a gift because her life decidedly revolved around neither romance nor motherhood, subjects too common and too often emphasized in portraying the lives of famous women. While Marcel shared her life, helping Roy with medical details, for example, in *The Cashier*, he clearly did not dominate it. After their first meal together, Dr. Carbotte drove the famous author home. In the following days, on numerous outings around Saint-Boniface and its environs, the two discovered a mutual interest in beautiful prairies, in long walks in the twilight (walking, in general, formed a habit they pursued often during their life together when Gabrielle's health permitted), and in each other. No great or all-consuming love match, Gabrielle and Marcel were more interested in a loving friendship, something each could supply the other: "Unconsciously, I was looking for a true friend in the world. So was he, very likely — and this we became to one another" (qtd. in Hind-Smith 89). Marcel, independent and successful in his own right, added the balance of warm companionship to Gabrielle's need for solitude and quiet. On 26 August 1947, after knowing each other for three months, they were married in Saint-Vital, where Anna and her family made their home. In her letter to Bernadette written at the beginning of their three-year stay in France, Gabrielle describes Marcel as "unusually thoughtful and sensitive" (22 Jan. 1948, *Letters* 11).

During their stay in France after the roar of the Prix Femina died down, Gabrielle returned to writing and also travelled to Brittany, Switzerland, and England while her husband pursued his medical studies. Most of the articles and short stories written during this period, including the stories mentioned earlier in conjunction with *The Cashier*, were inspired by France and by her travels. "The rest," she wrote to Bernadette, "on the other hand, have been dictated by homesickness" (13 June 1949, *Letters* 16). François Ricard suggests that while "Saint-Anne-la-Palud" and "La Camargue," two articles that were first published in 1951 and 1952 and later reprinted in *The Fragile Lights of Earth*, do derive from Roy's experiences in France, her reference in the letter to work dictated by homesickness may well refer to *Where Nests the Water Hen* (*Letters* 202 n25).

Roy's profound capacity to articulate certain shared but infrequently acknowledged human responses is evident in the sentiments she expressed in one of her letters to Bernadette, written during her stay in France: "Distance stirs curious feelings inside us. It awakens affection for many things we never knew we loved. From here, I can see how incomparably beautiful, youthful, and dynamic life is in Canada" (13 June 1949, *Letters* 17). And so from France, Gabrielle and Marcel returned to Ville LaSalle, a suburb of Montreal, in June of

1950. In 1952 they established their permanent residence in Quebec City on Grande-Allée, moving only once more before Gabrielle's death — upstairs to a larger apartment with a better view. Roy loved Canada, Quebec in particular, and felt that she, like the salmon, followed her parents' movement but in the opposite direction. Looking back in 1979, she wrote that, without Quebec, she would not have been the writer she was. Indeed, she did not know what she would have become without Quebec; she owed everything to that province ("Lettre de Gabrielle Roy" 102).

Insulated by her husband, her lawyer, and later by her publisher, Alain Stanké, from irksome distractions, Gabrielle spent the rest of her life writing, transposing reality into fiction. Dogged by constant fatigue, until her death from heart failure on 13 July 1983, Roy suffered numerous physical complaints: stomach ailments, goitre, hyperthyroidism, sinusitis, chronic neuritis in her eye, sneezing fits, insomnia, and, worst of all, foot problems (she had an operation on her left foot in 1970). Roy loved walking — whether on the prairies, in forests, in city slums; whether in France, Greece, Florida, Manitoba, or Quebec — and during her walks she jotted down notes on pieces of paper she crammed into her pockets. For Gabrielle some form of movement — whether on foot or swinging in her hammock at her summer home in Petite-Rivière-Saint-François — was integral to her artistic inspiration. Thus, to have foot problems was the unkindest cut of all. As she told Donald Cameron, "The thoughts that have any worth come to me as I walk, as I move" (143).

In later life, however, nothing was more fragile than her nerves. The following letter to Bernadette, written on 2 July 1965 and here reprinted in its entirety, speaks volumes about Roy's need to live a life safe from intrusions and/or interruptions from the outside world:

> Chère petite soeur,
> I'm writing you in haste about your "petition" on behalf of Sister Henri-de-Marie. I really would like to oblige

FIGURE 19

*Vista from Marcel and Gabrielle's summer
cottage at Petite-Rivière-Saint-François.*

her and at the same time do you a favour. It won't be easy. Anyway, I don't plan to be in Quebec City between the dates you've given me. It's always difficult to know beforehand when I'm going to be in town — if at all — during the summer. The simplest thing would be of course for Sister Henri to come to Petite-Rivière, but I can't put her up and the village has no hotel facilities. If her cousin could drive her here I could probably give her an hour or two, not really more. Strange as it may seem, it's during the summer holidays that I have most to do. But I think I could give her a little time, particularly in the afternoon, provided she tells me when she's coming at least four or five days before, and at that time gives me an address where I can reach her in case it becomes necessary to call it off; best of all a telephone number where I can leave a message for her.

All things considered, I think the best time for her to come would be while you and Clémence are here, because afterwards I may be going somewhere else for a few weeks. I'm sorry not to be able to do better and hope this will fit in with the time Sister Henri has free.

Rest well. Have you received the Equanil I had the drugstore send you?

A big hug to you till I have the joy of giving you a real one. (*Letters* 78)

A little clarification may be in order. Gabrielle and Marcel had bought a summer cottage in 1957 in Petite-Rivière-Saint-François in the county of Charlevoix on the north shore of the Saint Lawrence River estuary, about sixty-five miles north of Quebec City. There she spent her summers alone or with Marcel, depending on his schedule, for the rest of her life. Following her first summer there, she described the vista from the summer house in a letter to Bernadette:

I really believe the view is one of the most beautiful in the world. From the top of a small cliff we overlook the river where it's very wide; on one side there's a line of lovely hills, and below us lies Ile-aux-Coudres, about midway between the two shores. Behind, we have a high mountain covered with maples and birches almost to its peak. A marvellous sight! (2 Oct. 1957, *Letters* 24)

Convent rules at that time regulated virtually every aspect of a nun's life; obtaining permission to vacation in an area other than one sanctioned by the Church was therefore no mean feat. So one can imagine that Bernadette, probably bubbling over with excitement at the prospect of visiting her sister at Petite-Rivière in the summer of 1965, attracted the attention of Sister Henri-de-Marie, who might have deemed it timely to solicit an interview via Bernadette with her famous sister for an article she intended to write. Viewed in this light, Gabrielle's letter in response to her sister's request throws up multiple roadblocks: she is out of town, her schedule is too busy and capricious, and she cannot be depended on to keep a rendezvous even if a date were set. Her desire to meet Sister Henri during Bernadette and Clémence's visit may well have been motivated by a foreknowledge that her sisters' visit meant Gabrielle would get little work done anyway and that their presence might also mitigate the anxiety of a one-on-one interview with someone she did not know. In an undated letter from this same month (July 1965), Roy mentions receiving a letter from Sister Henri and asks Bernadette to serve as an intermediary. Apparently this incident had a happy ending, because Sister Henri eventually did interview Gabrielle at Petite-Rivière; Gabrielle even later questioned her sister about whether Sister Henri had enjoyed her visit (3 Dec. 1965, *Letters* 83). Many who desired interviews met with less luck, for Roy relished her privacy and found interviews extremely taxing.

Remembering the teenager who was so ardent in her studies that her mother unscrewed fuses to force her to get sufficient sleep, empathetic readers who feel equally driven will easily understand the anxiety that interruptions provoke in those who work not over the course of a day with frequent breaks

FIGURE 20

*Bernadette (left), Clémence, and Gabrielle at the time of
the sisters' reunion at Petite-Rivière-Saint-François in 1965.*

but who labour intensely for hours at a time with no breaks. For *The Tin Flute*, Roy typed continuously during the morning and early afternoon hours without stopping, writing eight to ten hours a day. The rest of the time she spent rehashing her day's work and anticipating the next day's efforts, often while taking a walk. For a writer of Gabrielle Roy's ilk, an interruption could change the course of her novel. In 1947, Roy freely admitted to Dorothy Duncan that "there are times when she can't meet people at all" (54), and in 1948 she wrote Bernadette, "I don't go out much, though, because nothing tires me more than social events. We [Gabrielle and Marcel] rarely accept invitations, and only when the hosts are people who genuinely like us" (13 June 1949, *Letters* 17).

PETITE-RIVIÈRE-SAINT-FRANÇOIS

Reclusive for professional reasons and by nature, Roy's assessment of her behaviour during her sisters' eventual visit to Petite-Rivière only confirms her need for solitude. As we have already seen, writing cheques soothed Roy's guilt over neglecting her family and obviated the need for personal involvement. She generously sent Bernadette and Clémence $500 to ensure that they could afford comfortable sleeping accommodations on the train and sent tranquillizers to help them enjoy a good night's sleep. However, to reach Petite-Rivière from Manitoba, Bernadette and Clémence had to change trains in Montreal and again in Quebec City. Once Gabrielle realized, with some frustration, that her sisters would arrive too late to make the second connection, she confirmed that she and Marcel would make the two-hour trip there to pick the two up. Hoping that her sisters could travel by train all the way to Roy's summer house is forgivable. On the other hand, in her undated July letter of 1965, Gabrielle must have been responding to the always perceptive Bernadette's suggestion that perhaps she and Clémence should shorten the projected length of their visit when she wrote in the opening sentence, "Yes, of course, you and Clémence will stay here as long as you can." But "here" does not translate into "here at *our* house"; "here" translates into Bernadette's assuming the bulk of responsibility for Clémence since the two would stay in a separate, although nearby, house. A second undated letter, meant for the departing sisters to open on the train back to Manitoba, reads as follows: "Forgive me if I snapped at you a bit at times. It was because of my nerves, you might say, because deep in my heart I was never in the least cross with you." To exonerate her behaviour further, she adds that she must resemble their father, a man given often to "scolding those he loved most" (*Letters* 80). In fairness to Gabrielle, some of her testiness may have been due to trying to finish *The Road Past Altamont*, which appeared in bookstores in the spring of 1966.

Once safely stowed on the return train to Manitoba, Bernadette and Clémence then reaped only Gabrielle's love, nostalgia for their presence, and longing for their return. Gabrielle probably truly enjoyed her sisters' visit, particularly in retrospect when their presence no longer made her feel anxious; regardless, she seems somewhat disingenuous in the following sampling of comments written subsequent to her sisters' visit: "For several days it was as though this beautiful, majestic countryside had nothing left to offer me. I couldn't pass 'your' little house, either, without feeling a tug at my heart" (16 Aug. 1965, *Letters* 80). "Who knows, perhaps there are several more happy meetings in store, like this summer's. I don't know if it was as perfect for you as it was for Marcel and me; if so it's almost a miracle" (3 Oct. 1965, *Letters* 82); in the same letter, Gabrielle gushes that Bernadette and Clémence will forever be a part of Petite-Rivière's landscape. "I keep remembering the magical times we spent together this summer. . . . Oh, if only this beautiful thing can happen to us once again in our lives!" (3 Dec. 1965, *Letters* 83). "[W]e must start dreaming of this now. . . . Maman will see to it from up there in heaven. . . . [O]ur souls . . . need a dream like this for nourishment" (5 Jan. 1966, *Letters* 87). Even in 1967, the memory of her sisters' visit apparently still moved Gabrielle: "I sometimes tell myself that perhaps we'll be lucky enough to have another get-together at Petite-Rivière" (5 Apr. 1967, *Letters* 96). "[F]or me Petite-Rivière is still so filled with incomparable memories of the summer you were here with Clémence. . . . If only it could all happen at least once more; this is my fervent hope" (6 June 1967, *Letters* 96).

Bernadette reacted enthusiastically, answering Gabrielle's letters in kind and proposing a second summer's holiday with Gabrielle in the East. But rather than responding with open arms and jubilation at the possibility of her sisters' return visit, Gabrielle, writing on 8 March 1969 from the warm sunshine at New Smyrna Beach, Florida, offered Bernadette nothing but obstacles: no longer any little house to rent for them, no precise dates, Marcel's plans and health uncertain, and Clémence's health and dietary restrictions complicating everything enormously. She even went so far as to suggest that Bernadette take Clémence to Kenora or some other restful place. Such a suggestion may strike the reader as being more than a bit unfair to Bernadette, saddled as she would be with a companion terribly difficult at times to understand and who, in Roy's words, "doesn't care much about living" (10 May 1947, *Letters* 7). On 30 June 1969, Gabrielle, having received only charming letters from both sisters, wrote again about the obstacles beyond her control that prevented her from hosting Bernadette and Clémence, suggesting again that the two take off for a few days together. As matters turned out, Bernadette, Clémence, and Antonia (their brother Germain's widow) did spend a holiday together at Victoria Beach, a resort on Lake Winnipeg. Gabrielle did not join them. Even had things worked out for another visit at Petite-Rivière, Roy wrote that she preferred that Bernadette and Clémence take their first two meals in their own lodgings, joining Gabrielle for supper "quietly" at her house (8 Mar. 1969, *Letters* 116). Gabrielle's desperation to avoid involvement with others was further underlined in her postscripts to this same letter. There she mentioned how she had avoided a possible television interview and also begged Bernadette not to intercede on behalf

FIGURE 21

In March 1970, Gabrielle spent three weeks with her beloved "Dédette," Sister Léon-de-la-Croix, in Saint-Boniface. Bernadette died 25 May 1970.

of any others seeking interviews with Gabrielle. We can only guess at Bernadette's reaction, but whatever it was, she probably willingly forgave Gabrielle. This gentle nun, who possessed the "tranquil joy of a soul at peace . . . [which she] spread to everyone around [her]" (1 Apr. 1947, *Letters* 6), seemed to understand her celebrated sister's easily frayed nerves.

Bernadette never paid another visit to the house at Petite-Rivière, for in 1970 she developed cancer and died that same year. That very summer, Roy, undone by the loss of Bernadette, began writing *Enchanted Summer*, a celebration of life, which she dedicated to her neighbour in Petite-Rivière, Berthe François; to her neighbours at Grande-Pointe; and to "the children of all seasons with the wish that they will never tire of listening to their planet earth"; but the spirit of Bernadette and her spontaneous joy at creation truly inspire the narrative. Several months after Bernadette's death and probably while Roy worked on *Enchanted Summer*, she dreamed of her departed sister:

She was back to life and she was very gay as she had been — full of life and full of spirit, and eager to live and see and hug as many things as possible, and she looked so happy to be back amongst the living, I couldn't get over it. She was just *racing* to everything — flowers and trees, and water and air, and she was just vibrating with the joy of finding herself back amongst the living, and telling me, You don't know how lucky you are! It's *wonderful* to be alive! The whole dream was very vivid: here was Dédette rushing like a bird to everything, trembling with joy. And I found myself crying and crying and crying, the tears were pouring down my face, and she was saying, Well, what are you crying for? I'm back! I'm alive! [I]t's so wonderful! I cried and I cried, and I woke up, and I thought, What am I crying about? because there was such *sadness* in my heart that it woke me up in tears. Well, I was crying because she was back

among the living — and she would have to die again.
(Cameron 137–38)

The description attests to Roy's affection for Dédette as much as it characterizes her own art; Gabrielle Roy in all her works, to recall a remark by Camus, offers a stirring tapestry of beauty and tragedy, striving always to ensure that the tragedy of life never hides its beauty and that the beauty never hides life's tragedy — in other words, to disclose human experience in all its enchantment and sorrow.

Grieving over the death of her much-loved sister and taking inspiration from her memory, Roy found solace in nature and its wondrous cycle of regeneration. As she told Joan Hind-Smith, "Every writer must eventually write his Ninth Symphony or give in to despair" (124). The stories in *Enchanted Summer* offer a chorus of nature's sounds and scents, underscoring both sisters' love of beauty and providing fitting testimony to the profound affection that developed between them over the years after their mother's death. And the manner in which Dédette's essential spirit, captured in Roy's vivid dream, permeates the narratives poignantly illustrates how Roy transformed experience into art; as she said, "the artistic creation is born of a dream that appears to be the source of all reality" (Delson-Karan 202; our translation).

CHILDREN OF THE HEART

In the 1970s Roy turned her hand to writing children's books: *Ma vache Bossie* (1976), *Court-queue* (1979), and *L'espagnole et la pékinoise* (published posthumously in 1986). From 1972 until the time of her death, Roy also published two more major works of fiction, *Garden in the Wind* (1975) and *Children of My Heart* (1977), which garnered her yet another Governor General's Award for Fiction. Written in Quebec, the works hearken back to Roy's years in Manitoba and on the Canadian prairies. Throughout this biography, we have called attention to how Roy's experiences prior to her becoming a successful author inspired and informed her work; how specific themes in her oeuvre developed from or find reference in her life; how Gabrielle Roy the artist created her fiction through the double sieve of art and experience; how after her greatest commercial success, *The Tin Flute*, Gabrielle retired from the public sphere to devote the remaining years of her life to writing, in effect separating herself from her fellow humans the better to know them. On her own terms, therefore, she did not escape her fellow humans — she embraced them. Roy came to view her books as "a gift equivalent" to the children she desired as a young woman, viewing these artistic creations as the significant facts and important events of her life (qtd. in Cobb 14). We now turn our attention to a brief look at these many children of her heart.

In her study of Gabrielle Roy, M.G. Hesse refers to a polarity Roy herself identified with respect to her major works: "first, an interest in the common people and everyday, contemporary life, and second, an interest in herself, in discovering herself" (11). Another polarity, although less exact, manifests itself in the settings in which her narratives unfold: cities, particularly major metropolitan areas, versus anything but cities — prairies, tundra, vast snow-and-ice-covered northern expanses of Canada, farms, rivers, isolated hinterlands. City settings are somewhat anomalous — antithetical to the rest of her work. *The Tin Flute* and *The Cashier*, in fact, are a group by themselves, and Roy abandons the city as a setting after the publication of *The Cashier* in 1954, except to relate Pierre Cadorai's experiences in Paris in *The Hidden Mountain* (1961).

The Tin Flute and *The Cashier*, faithful in their realistic depictions of the life of slum dwellers and of a bank teller, cannot help but be overshadowed by the sense of absurdity germane to the life of city dwellers. *The Tin Flute*, told in a sequence of chapters that represent in themselves fairly complete narrative pieces, betraying perhaps the novel's original conception as a series of articles, chronicles the lives of an impoverished family in the Montreal slum of Saint-Henri. The stories of the forever house-searching and pregnant (again!) mother, Rose-Anna, and of her pretty, looking-for-escape-through-marriage daughter, Florentine, form the nexus of a claustrophobic narrative that treats in detail over a period of three months (from February to May of 1940) the stagnant lives of all the members of this needy family at the height of the Great Depression. The disturbing ending posits salvation in the guise of war. The ne'er-do-well father and the eldest son eventually find long-term employment in the military, and Florentine, pregnant by a man she loved passionately, waves good-bye to her middle-class husband whom she does not love as he, too, leaves to perform his military duty. They are too blind and, perhaps, too poor to understand that war provides only a temporary solution to their destitution and that conditions could easily worsen; thereafter, the characters' naïve hope in the abomination and atrocity of war elicits an uncomfortable pity from the reader. Roy does, however, register sharp social criticism, having one poverty-stricken character remark acidly, for instance, about the lack of money in Saint-Henri, "There was never enough for old age insurance, never enough for the schools or for orphans, never enough to give everybody a job. But look here, there's money enough for war" (102).

Despite The Tin Flute's depiction of a particular family's indigence, the novel draws its strength from this very situation's universality. The awards the novel attracted derive certainly from its considerable artistic merits, but equally as important, critics laud it for changing the course of the French Canadian novel, pulling it up, if you will, from its deeply embedded pastoral roots. As we noted, the novel's immediate success paralysed Roy for some time. While she clearly recovered, she nonetheless felt that The Tin Flute contained many imperfections and that her later works were far superior. But Roy took considerable pride in the fact that the novel ultimately had such a profound impact on the direction of French Canadian literature: "I created a ground-breaking work" (Delson-Karan 200; our translation).

FIGURE 22

Publicity photo of Roy taken in 1955 at the age of forty-six.

Although a realistic novel detailing the intimate and exceedingly mundane, boring existence of a bank teller may sound unappealing, readers of *The Cashier* know how fast one turns the pages, so compelling is Roy's portrait of mediocre little Alexandre Chenevert. Even the thirty or so pages devoted to the man's protracted death from cancer fascinate as opposed to repel. Roy renders Chenevert's financial problems, his suffering, his guilt, his shouldering of the world's problems even more pathetic by illustrating his helplessness, alienation, and anonymity in the daily life of a busy metropolis. As we noted earlier, Roy undertook *The Cashier* in 1947 while in France but abandoned it temporarily to write the rather utopian *Where Nests the Water Hen*. In Chenevert's case, his dreams of universal solidarity and fraternity, instead of ennobling him, only accentuate his isolation, enclosed as he is in his glass teller's cage at the bank.

Chenevert permits himself and the reader a pastoral interlude in the middle of the novel, framed by the opening section that enumerates almost painfully his daily life and the end that chronicles his prolonged illness, existential dread, and eventual death from cancer. Cancer, with its insidious ability to spread throughout the human body because normal cells do not recognize malignant cells as harmful, forms a wrenching metaphor in *The Cashier*. Even when given a chance to reassess his own raison d'être and perhaps to formulate plans to improve his life during a stay in the beautiful setting at Lac Vert in the Laurentian Mountains, Chenevert cannot shed his previous identity — though the reader might desire such a transformation, the author does not deal in miracles. During this holiday, he meets the LeGardeur family, who proclaim their happiness, and he admires the family's self-sufficiency, a product of their own labour. Inspired by the LeGardeurs, Chenevert nonetheless fails to recognize the hardships they have endured, seeing this family instead as relatives of the Golden Age shepherds who populate the fictive land of Arcadia. Chenevert likewise fails to acknowledge his own inability to survive in such an environment.

Strangely enough, the bank teller returns early from his vacation; somehow the peace and tranquillity of the sylvan setting prove less satisfying than the hassles — some of them self-induced! — of daily life in Montreal. When he becomes ill after his return, Chenevert challenges the very inadequate hospital chaplain to explain the meaninglessness of life; ironically, in the end, the actions of his acquaintances, providing answers that had always lain within his grasp, open his eyes to the potential for greatness in human beings and reconcile his vision of God. The conclusion provides Chenevert with a mantle of dignity, for as Roy marvelled, "It would have been so easy . . . for that little man to give up" (qtd. in Marshall 40); his perseverance becomes his great triumph, for the efforts lead him to appreciate the power of one human being's love for another.

Where Nests the Water Hen appeared in 1950, four years before *The Cashier*, and surprised Roy's readers by its radical contrast to *The Tin Flute*. Nevertheless, the book's arrival announced a trend in Roy's oeuvre that would find its culmination in *Enchanted Summer* (1972), the narrative inspired by Bernadette. The ideas for *Where Nests the Water Hen*, as we described, came to Roy while on a drive with friends to the beautiful Chartres Cathedral in France and a later stay at Epping Forest. The novel takes its basis in fact from two of Roy's earlier experiences, her teaching at the Little Water Hen and a visit during a summer break from teaching with her cousin Eliane, her Uncle Excide's eldest daughter, at Camperville on the edge of Lake Winnipegosis. Eliane had six children, and to keep herself busy Roy gave lessons to the three eldest. Just as Mademoiselle Côté does in the novel, Roy took the children swimming during the hot afternoon hours. In addition, Eliane's five-and-a-half year old, Denise, inspired little Joséphine of *Water Hen*, and Eliane's expressive eyes were models for Luzina's eyes — Luzina's name, of course, comes from the much-admired mother of Eliane. During this visit, Roy wrote during the morning hours, even trying her hand at Indian legends, all in search of her own writing style and genre.

With *Where Nests the Water Hen* Roy discovered her creative niche. In contrast to the realism and desire to tell it as it was in *The Tin Flute* and *The Cashier*, Roy preferred "to break up the elements of [her] own experience, separate them, reassemble them, add to them, leave this or that out and perhaps invent things" (*Enchantment* 87). Readers of Roy's works should therefore avoid taking the elements of her first-person narratives and construing them as autobiographical facts. As she wrote in her autobiography, composed in the 1970s, "It would bore me to death now to describe a house faithfully just as I see it, or a street or a corner bar, the way I did in *The Tin Flute*" (*Enchantment* 87). Roy never forsook reality in her observation and characterization, but her goal was not realism for realism's sake as much as the evocation of a mood.

In *Where Nests the Water Hen* — itself in some respects a prelapsarian response to the fallen worlds of *The Tin Flute* and *The Cashier*, and perhaps, in part, a reaction as well to the destruction she witnessed in postwar Europe — Roy evokes a terrestrial paradise, a large, loving family, living on a beautiful island in the middle of a river and raising sheep, isolated from other human beings and civilization. Although the narrative certainly accents the idyllic, this paradise also offers swarms of mosquitoes, harsh winters, a nasty landlord, and boredom. Likewise, the children eventually grow and relocate in the cities of Canada, where they earn their living and speak English; and Father Joseph-Marie must intercede to protect the halfbreed traders from the unscrupulous store owner, Bessette, to ensure that they receive their fair share, only to watch them spend their dollars on liquor and further enrich the merchant: "These wretched halfbreeds, exploited from their very origins, were still exploited by all sorts of pleasure-vendors who took advantage of their innocence. They were not equipped to handle too much money, not being used to money's ways" (132). By defining utopia in *Water Hen* as an environment responding to the physical and emotional needs of its inhabitants, the novelist could easily perpetrate a myth of harmony, but Roy underscores the Little Water Hen's

FIGURE 23

*The Roy house in Saint-Boniface was sold in the early 1930s.
This picture, taken in 1982, shows that the house was subject
to change — a theme that haunts Roy's oeuvre.*

obvious restrictions in relationship to the outside world while extolling its potential.

Despite her Paris publisher's displeasure with the new direction in her writing, which lacked the political and social ethos of the *engagé(e)*, and despite the relative failure in Quebec of this work, English-speaking Canada loved it; the novel became a popular school text. In the throes of defining its own identity, this part of Canada felt that *Where Nests the Water Hen* reaffirmed the heritage of its pioneers and the essence of the pioneers' relationship to the land. In 1970 Roy signed an agreement with Canada's National Film Board, which made a multimedia presentation (slides, film footage, and drawings) in both English and French ("Of Many People" or "Un siècle d'hommes") based on *Where Nests the Water Hen* for Manitoba's centennial celebrations.

Where Nests the Water Hen, an apparent aberration, book-ended as it was by the Montreal novels, *The Tin Flute* and *The Cashier*, actually served as a turning point, announcing the dominant course of the rest of her oeuvre, in which she would write about what moved her the most: herself, her family, her travels, foreign settlers, and children. The book also encapsulates Roy's particular narrative artistry: a series of stories, loosely unified in time and space, collected together. Such a genre escapes the usual designation of "novel" and has yet to find a literary designation in its own right. Nevertheless, *Where Nests the Water Hen* anticipates the structure revealed in most of her remaining works. Only *The Tin Flute*, *The Cashier*, and *The Hidden Mountain* fulfil the basic criteria readers usually associate with novels.

In 1956 the Prix Duvernay was awarded to Roy for her combined literary achievement in and contribution to French literature. In 1957 Roy received her second Governor General's Award, for the English edition of *Street of Riches*, first published in Montreal in 1955. *Street of Riches*, stories inspired by her childhood and her family, may have sparked the beginning of Adèle's long-sustained animosity toward her sister. Adèle, too, had written a work based on the Roy family history;

Gabrielle's work far outclassed that of her jealous sister and, by 1962, had become another school text. In terms of Roy's personal literary development, *Street of Riches*, by repeating and further cultivating the structure she adopted in *Where Nests the Water Hen*, and building on what François Ricard aptly calls "the autobiographical imagination," confirmed the orientation of many future literary creations by Roy ("Métamorphose" 453; our translation). The first-person recounting of childhood memories by Christine in *Street of Riches* announces the demise of the urban-based narrative as found in *The Tin Flute* and *The Cashier*. Appearing merely a year and a half after *The Cashier*, *Street of Riches* seems to have been written with the same relative ease and fervour as *Where Nests the Water Hen*, and it remains a significant literary achievement in the history of Roy's development as one of Canada's most important contemporary writers. If *The Tin Flute* was the first Canadian novel to speak on behalf of Montreal's poor, *Street of Riches* gave voice for the first time to those who inhabit the rather insular, French-speaking world of Saint-Boniface and other similar islands of French that dot the Canadian prairie. Indeed, the French edition, *Rue Deschambault*, takes its title from the very street on which the Roy family lived. Readers of this novel will easily detect in the narrator an echo of Gabrielle Roy the author, who, writing the stories in Quebec, drew on her experiences prior to "escaping" from Saint-Boniface for this showcase of her autobiographical imagination. Christine the schoolteacher, at the conclusion of the narratives her memories have inspired, says, "I did not fully realize it yet — often our joys are slow in coming home to us — but I was living through one of the rarest happinesses of my life." (246).

Often linked with *Street of Riches*, but separated from it by the publication of *The Hidden Mountain*, is another semi-autobiographical account of Roy's childhood experiences in Manitoba, *The Road Past Altamont* (1966). Also a collection of stories linked by the first-person narrator Christine, *The Road Past Altamont* confirms the direction of her work throughout the 1960s and 1970s, including "My Manitoba Heritage" (1970, reprinted in *The Fragile Lights of Earth*), *Enchanted Summer* (1972), *Children of My Heart* (1977), and her autobiography *Enchantment and Sorrow* (1984).

Despite its similarities to *Street of Riches* — including the same narrator, Christine, and experiences gained from growing up on the prairies — *The Road Past Altamont* exceeds the former in depth and insight. The Christine of *Street of Riches* relates many of the incidents from the perspective of a child, a sort of interpretation à la Huckleberry Finn of French Canadian life on the prairies, and the book concludes with Christine as a young woman on the brink of adulthood during her first year as a teacher. *The Road Past Altamont*, particularly the title story, maintains the mature perspective of a reminiscing adult who attempts to understand the child she once was and who ventures as well to recapture the magic of childhood her adult vision of the world has muddled. Within these parameters, Roy explores "the relationships between generations and the cyclical continuity of life" (Grosskurth 51). Taken together, *The Road Past Altamont* and *Street of Riches* offer, through an examination of Christine's growth in relation to Gabrielle Roy's achievement, "a 'portrait of the artist as a young woman,' or, at least, of the values and motivation that will be central to [Roy] as a writer" (Socken, "In Memoriam" 108). The four stories in *The Road Past Altamont* detail the child Christine's relationship with her grandmother and with a neighbouring old man, the adult Christine's relationship with her mother, and the child's disillusionment after her experiences with a poor family's relocation from a dilapidated house outside of town to one equally disreputable in a run-down part of town, demystifying forever in her imagination the idea that a move is a wonderful adventure. Through these tales, *The Road Past Altamont* offers a mature meditation on themes that reappear in all of Roy's works — appearance versus reality, death versus renewal, rupture versus integration, and progress versus tradition, especially as the last affects French Canadians. Roy leads us to a more mature understanding of these universal polarities by giving them artistic coherence and by developing them in the context of common human experience. Indeed, *The Road Past Altamont* marks an end to the quest for identity by both the narrator Christine and Roy herself. In her later works, with a few exceptions, Roy turns her attention instead to the tangled lives of others, although as usual without any attempt at resolution but always with an empathy that brings solace to all of us who are often perplexed by life's unexpected turns.

The thoughtful story of a young girl's trying to come to terms with ageing and death, among other issues, seems to have captured the public's imagination, for Roy wrote a screenplay based on "The Old Man and the Child" for Radio Canada. Owing to a lack of funds, however, and because she "wrote it as a short feature film and they wanted a full-length film," no film was made during her lifetime (Delson-Karan 201). In 1986, thanks to a new adaptation by Claude Grenier of the National Film Board, the film did appear three years after Gabrielle Roy's death.

Apparently Bernadette also took special pleasure from *The Road Past Altamont*. In letters to her famous sister, she wrote glowing accounts of her communion with nature during annual vacations at a religious camp on Lake Winnipeg, and these may have inspired some of the descriptions of the lake that appear in "The Old Man and the Child," a story about the young Christine's first trip to that lake. Gabrielle wrote to Bernadette that she hoped her sister's enjoyment of Lake Winnipeg and its environs would be all the greater for having read the story (7 June 1966, *Letters* 92). From Roy's responses to Bernadette's letters, we may conclude that nature evoked similar sentiments in the sisters. Roy believed that she was united with Bernadette, Mélina, and their father (with his love for roses and birds) in their general delight in summer and in nature, but that Bernadette "had no equal for helping the rest of us see things we often miss though they're right before our eyes" (22 July 1964, *Letters* 97). The same could be said about the particular group of stories presented to the reading public in *Enchanted Summer*.

Published in 1972, only two years after Bernadette's death, *Enchanted Summer* consists of brief anecdotes about Gabrielle's summer experiences at her home in Petite-Rivière, with the exception of one story about her first day as a teacher in Marchand in 1929. Roy bases so many of the stories in this collection on the local flora, cows, frogs, and birds (the latter testifying to Roy's avid interest in bird watching) that human beings play almost a secondary role. Without any of Bernadette's summer letters surviving, one cannot help but wonder if, just as Roy distils so many of her own experiences, she does not also distil some of her sister's rapture into this enchanting work.

As is usual in Roy's work, even the portrait of an almost paradise is haunted by the presence of pain, sorrow, and death. The story of her first day as a teacher in Marchand, for example, completely out of sync in time and place with the rest of the work, tells of a child who died the previous evening. But Roy knew what she was doing. In a great writer, breaking a pattern announces itself as important, not as incompetence. One of the hallmarks of Roy the author is the intermingling of joy with sorrow and sorrow with joy. As she wrote to Bernadette about the implacable laws of nature:

> Now that I have a bit of a garden, I see how many enemies of all kinds there are for anything that lives. . . . What seems to us at first so peaceful and calm is in truth subject to merciless laws of nature — which is as it should be, no doubt. (23 June 1960, *Letters* 32)

Her "double" vision is, however, neither optimistic nor pessimistic; Roy simply finds manifested in the natural world the simultaneous oppositions people experience in their daily lives. And just as surely as death forms part of the natural cycle, death in nature precipitates regeneration and rebirth. From her realistic interpretation of the world around her, Roy thus draws hope.

FIGURE 24

Marcel and Gabrielle in Greece in 1963.

Petite-Rivière-Saint-François served as a pastoral retreat from the city for Roy, although in one letter to Bernadette she complained that the sea air that had refreshed her for years — most recently during a brief stay in the seaside village of Morbihan, France, in 1955 (4 June 1955, *Letters* 23) — tired her out and gave her palpitations (2 Oct. 1957, *Letters* 24). Regardless of her health, at their summer home Gabrielle and Marcel dedicated themselves to gardening, and Gabrielle to writing. Apparently, swinging in the porch hammock was as inspiring as walking, for she would often jump up to write several pages after a few minutes of repose. In the same letter in which she complained of the sea air, Roy added, "I've worked a great deal this summer, but so far I'm not pleased with what I've done" (*Letters* 25). Between *Street of Riches* in 1955 and *The Hidden Mountain* in 1961, Roy did not publish any books, and so these may have been anxious years for her. But always her own worst critic, Roy actually produced excellent material during this time between publications. In a note referring to the preceding letter to Bernadette, François Ricard writes that during this time Roy worked on stories based on her memories and family history, "some of which were published later as *La route d'Altamont* (*The Road Past Altamont*) in 1966 and *De quoi t'ennuies-tu, Eveline?* in 1982" (*Letters* 203 n35).

In addition to writing, from the late 1950s through the 1970s Roy, like so many of her characters, continued to travel for family concerns, for business, and for holidays. The influence of these travels can be seen in *The Hidden Mountain* (1961), *Windflower* (1970), and *Garden in the Wind* (1975). In 1955, Roy travelled to Saskatchewan, and in 1958 she journeyed to Manitoba to assure herself that Clémence was well cared for. (Over the ensuing years, she made numerous trips west to take care of Clémence's needs.) In 1957, she travelled with the artist René Richard and his wife to the southern United States; Richard, to whom Roy dedicated *The Hidden Mountain*, provided the model for the novel's protagonist, Pierre Cadorai. In 1960, she spent time at Cape Cod with a friend, and in 1961 she went north to Ungava, a peninsula in northern Quebec

FIGURE 25

Roy flanked on her right by the artist René Richard and on her left by Félix-Antoine Savard, priest, educator, and writer.

FIGURE 26

*Roy with René Richard, the artist and trapper
who was Roy's inspiration for Pierre Cadorai,
the protagonist of* The Hidden Mountain.

where she observed in her perceptive way some of the Eskimo experience, which would later translate into *Windflower*. Indicative of the manner in which Roy conflates various memories from different times and places into her work, this novel also draws on a wartime trip Roy made to Alaska, where, as she was getting off the plane, she saw an Eskimo woman holding a blond, blue-eyed baby:

> I thought the child was a product of a wartime romance with an American G.I. The image of the mother and child remained with me and haunted me. It turned out to be the source of inspiration for the creation of this novel. (Delson-Karan 203)

Her brother Germain's fatal car accident in 1961 brought her back for a sad visit to Saint-Boniface, where she spent time with Anna, Clémence, and Bernadette. From September to October 1961, she accompanied her husband to a medical convention in Vienna. Her next trip was to Greece, where she fell in love with the ruins and found the sunsets unparalleled by any except those she had beheld from her brother Jos's front porch at his house in Saskatchewan. In 1964 Roy went to Arizona to visit her dying sister, Anna, and stayed most of the month of January until after Anna's funeral. Aside from various trips to France, Roy began in 1968, a year before her sixtieth birthday, to spend her winters in sunny Florida, which seemed to improve her health and bring her ease. Thus, despite her relative reclusiveness, Roy's life was hardly confined to a cork-lined bedroom à la Marcel Proust but afforded her much travel and contact with the outside world when she felt so inclined.

In *The Hidden Mountain*, Roy's *ars poetica*, she writes so evocatively of the frozen North's vast expanses that the novel seems almost painted. Roy's quest for herself had ended, if such a quest ever truly ends, with *The Road Past Altamont*. *The Hidden Mountain* portrays allegorically the meaning Roy attributed to the artist's quest for perfection: "that of a long road towards an unobtainable ideal, but of which the artist could never abandon his or her pursuit without renouncing at the same time the very value on which the pursuit is based" (Ricard, "Le cercle" 75; our translation). And perhaps because Roy "paints" the life of Pierre Cadorai as he canoes, snowshoes, and dogsleds himself across the Northwest Territories into northern Quebec, all the while sketching and drawing with whatever implements he can lay hands on, this novel elicits a particularly Canadian sense of the artist. One critic even suggests an analogy between Cadorai and *The Cashier*'s citified Chenevert, pointing out that both men are in search of "a goal they do not comprehend" (Grosskurth 44).

Not much really happens in *The Hidden Mountain*: Cadorai travels, traps, and draws, travels, traps, and draws until he confronts a mountain, remote and yet sublime, in the Ungava region of northern Quebec. Like the "orders" to write that Gabrielle Roy described herself as receiving, Pierre feels compelled to capture the mountain with his art:

> Beyond all ordinary things I am beautiful; that is true, it was saying. As mountains go, I am perhaps the finest achievement of creation. Perhaps there is no other like me. However, since until now no man has seen me, did I in truth exist? (83)

He subsequently attempts to translate the mountain's beauty into brushstrokes on canvas but can only do so piecemeal, never capturing the mountain's essence in its entirety. Eventually Pierre earns a scholarship to Paris, but harnessing his instinctive talent to learn technique stifles his ability and tries his patience. And the works of the great masters hanging in the Louvre leave him thoroughly discouraged. Roy, herself hardly iconoclastic, maintains a delicate balance in her juxtaposition of the masters' technical brilliance and Pierre's natural talent, not promoting one over the other. Roy herself experienced an arduous search for an artistic path suitable for the stories she longed to tell, a search complicated by public acclaim and her need for financial security, as well as her shock at the machinations behind commercial publicity and literary awards, most of which ignore artistic merit. *The Hidden Mountain* helps to explain Roy's reclusiveness and the incompatibility artists often feel with the world around them.

On a deeper level, Roy exposes the artist's endeavour as one of the most damning, tragic quests. In the same way that Pierre Cadorai could never get his beloved mountain exactly right on canvas until just before his death, so the artistic pursuit of the ideal, the sublime, that final statement once and for all, remains forever out of reach or even frustratingly just out of reach, prodding the artist to try over and over again. As Roy explained, comparing her own writing with Pierre's painting, the author always has one more book to write:

> I think a writer dreams, as Pierre of *The Hidden Mountain* hoped, of putting all the subjects, briefly, in one undertaking. Of course he never arrives there, and that is why there are always writers and always artists. They're all chasing the one thing. Mauriac had a very beautiful expression: he said that he was always striving to write the one book that would dispense him from writing others. Fundamentally what we hope is to get it all down in one book, or in one picture, or in one song, but of course always something is left out. That's why we start again. (Cameron 144)

This philosophy is well suited to Gabrielle Roy, who was doomed by her ability to see both sides of a question, never finding or crafting single-faceted jewels of truth about the human condition but revealing instead a kaleidoscope of human experience, multifaceted, equivocal, and complex. The pursuit of the impossible, always posited in the imagination as possible, lends dignity and nobility to the painter's and the writer's ongoing attempts to attain perfection. To the extent that the narrative concerns a person seeking truth and meaning in life, *The Hidden Mountain* addresses a dilemma particular to more than just artists. On one hand, as Gabrielle Roy states, the novel "is about every [person] who aspires"; on the other hand, like *The Cashier*, *The Hidden Mountain* possesses serious religious overtones, for as Roy said of Pierre, "He is in the hands of the Creator. The Creator is always above him" (qtd. in Hind-Smith 109).

Roy's last major publication other than her autobiography was inspired by memories of the special relationships she enjoyed with her students. *Children of My Heart* (1977) offers six stories about six different and special children she taught during her years at Cardinal and at the Académie Provencher. As is usual in Roy's work, the autobiographical element must give way to the artistic. In *Children of My Heart*, for example, the stories are not presented in chronological order. Indeed, the *last* story treats her first year at Cardinal, nearly fifty years in the past, while the *first* story concerns a mature, experienced teacher prepared for and anticipating the gamut of reactions of her little students on the first day of school. The simple disruption of chronological order in itself skews the autobiographical elements.

Much as these stories focus on the various personalities and/or aptitudes of children Roy may or may not have taught — the Ukrainian Nil's singing, which disarms even the most cynical listener, the gentle Clair's almost religious devotion to those he loves, the adolescent Médéric's awakening to erotic love — these separate texts also highlight the teacher's sensitivity to the children and her interest in nurturing their unique qualities. Readers thus confront not Roy's actual experiences but her vision of an ideal derived from the daily and at times tragic life of immigrant populations — their poverty and ignorance; how real-life concerns force children to interrupt or cease their education because their labour is required elsewhere; the brutality, physical and psychological, that children come to know at a very early age.

Against such overwhelming odds, as harsh as winter on the Canadian prairies, *Children of My Heart* counters with the value of education and the singular significance of one of the most comprehensive and complex emotions: love. As the stories attest, the children for whom one feels the most hope are those who experience love, and, for the most part, maternal love. Fathers do not fare well in the stories, except for those who are absent or for the passionate Italian father in the first story of the collection, "Vincento." About this one emotion, Roy does not prevaricate. Her vision of the ideal power of love derives its strength from being filtered through the harsh lens of the real. Thus, the beautiful and erotic attraction of the adolescent student, Médéric, for his teacher, herself only four years older than the Métis boy, expresses the author's belief "that the strongest and deepest love that one ever experiences is that first passion in one's life, the love of a pupil for a teacher" (Lewis, "Last" 210). But beauty is sullied by village gossip and Médéric's tyrannical father. Even so, the tender attraction the teacher and the boy share overpowers the tragedy and remains with the reader. This particular story highlights Roy's ability to unearth the ideal from within the deep and often hidden roots of the real, a hallmark of her talent.

Windflower, published in 1970, comprised of three short stories and a novella, makes for some intriguing and, at times, delightful reading. In essence a portrayal of the tug between the Eskimo way of life and the influence of white people's civilization, Windflower remains poised on a seesaw, never touching ground in favour of either civilization, each with its own drawbacks and integrity. The short stories, somewhat comic in presentation, especially the one about the Eskimo Barnaby's experiences with a telephone, nevertheless speak to serious concerns about the confrontation between the two cultures. Especially poignant are two stories about sick Eskimos. White civilization, with its fear of death and its emphasis on prolonging life no matter what the cost, looks silly in comparison with the Eskimo acceptance of and provisions for death, such as their practice of exposing the old and ailing to the elements. But whites make the Eskimos ashamed of their lack of a proper (that is, white) reverence for life. Eskimo culture in turn questions the whites' sometimes incongruous efforts to prolong human life. Life confined to a wheelchair? Perhaps. But to a wheelchair on the tundra? Essentially the answer to the question of which culture respects life more does not flatter modern advances. Judgements about the respective cultures serve to deepen readers' perceptions of their own way of life. The novella about the Eskimo woman, Elsa, raped by an American soldier and trying subsequently to give her half-white son the best life possible, leaves the reader with strong feelings of being caught in a trap. Coping alternately with the demands made on her and her child by two very different cultures, Elsa attempts to raise her son first one way and then the other, all at great cost to herself. Victimized from the beginning to the end of the story, Elsa's one glory is her unfounded belief in her runaway son's success in the military, a success or failure that her son, selfish or victimized himself, will never return to confirm.

Garden in the Wind, perhaps more than any other work, and in a manner more direct than her memories captured in essence rather than in fact in *Street of Riches*, *The Road Past Altamont*, *The Hidden Mountain*, and *Children of My Heart*, gives voice to previously mute and at times rootless immigrants. "The Vagabond," which could be considered a metaphor for Roy's art and its significance, is a story about telling stories and about the importance of ensuring that people remember and translate human experience as well as hear this experience recounted orally. "The Houdou Valley," comic, ironic, satiric, sympathetic, derives from Roy's father's stories of his work and her own experiences with immigrant populations during her travels as a journalist. Portraying the hopefulness of these groups in their resettlement in a sort of "promised land," Roy, as usual, punctures the dreams with reality but never deflates them completely. One of Roy's better known stories, "Where Will You Go Sam Lee Wong?" transcribes the thoughts of her most mute character. Finally, in "A Garden at the End of the World," Roy records the life of a lonely, misunderstood, ageing wife, miles away from any vestige of civilization, whose only joy is her garden, despite the incredible physical pain she endures to tend it.

Throughout all her narratives, Roy aims to depict the ordinary, although at times shockingly desolate, lives that common, generally good people across Canada share. She gives voice to the traditionally voiceless and makes vibrant the drab patterns of their existence, ennobling their endeavours simply by articulating them as subjects worthy of art. The presence of harsh reality in practically all of her writing serves only to create tales more genuine, more poignant, more true to the lives her characters live. Life is full of anguish and distress, and Roy acknowledges the pain. At the same time that readers experience this pain, they also uncover solace in Roy's works, solace that derives not from the reality of human sorrow but from the gentleness in her presentation. As Gabrielle Roy said near the end of her life, "What counts the most for me is human tenderness" (Delson-Karan 204; our translation). She delves into her own experiences and projects her individual sorrow and enchantment onto a screen of human existence that, remarkably, speaks to us all.

Roy promises her readers no silver lining but reveals instead an essential aspect of the whole, in all the wonderfulness of its confusions, detours, false promises, and mirages. In response to the mother's bleak depiction of the future as "a terrible thing" or as "something of a defeat" in Street of Riches, Christine writes:

> But I still hoped that I could have everything: both a warm and true life, like a shelter — at times, too, unbearable with harsh truth — and also time to capture its reverberation in the depths of the soul; time to wake, and time to halt that I might understand; time to withhold myself a little along the road, and then to catch up with the others, to rejoin them and to cry joyously, "Here I am, and here is what I've found for you along the way!" (209)

Her works continue to beckon us as quiet documents of the Canadian mosaic, infused with hope — hope for the powerless, the marginal, the indigent, the disenfranchised; hope for a kinder human race; hope for a united Canada. Truly, a store of riches awaits the uninitiated reader. As Gabrielle Roy herself wrote: "Here I am, and look what I've found for you along the way! . . . Have you waited for me? . . . Aren't you waiting for me? . . . Oh, do wait for me! . . ." (*Street* 209).

CHRONOLOGY

(All dates for Roy's works refer to their original publication in French.)

1909   Gabrielle Roy born in Saint-Boniface, Manitoba, on 22
        March to Mélina Landry Roy (age forty-two) and Léon Roy
        (age fifty-nine). Gabrielle is the youngest of eleven children,
        eight of whom survive past adolescence.

1911   Conservative candidate Robert Borden defeats Prime Min-
        ister Wilfrid Laurier, whom Léon Roy idolizes.

1913   For reasons connected with his continued support of Laur-
        ier, the Canadian government fires Léon Roy from his job
        as a Federal Settlement Officer, depriving him of his pen-
        sion and casting the family into near poverty.

1927   Roy completes secondary studies at Académie Saint-Joseph
        in Saint-Boniface, winning numerous awards for her pro-
        ficiency in French and in English. In September she enters
        Winnipeg Normal Institute to earn her teaching credential.

1929   Léon Roy dies on 20 February. Gabrielle graduates from
        Winnipeg Normal Institute and takes her first teaching
        assignment at Marchand for one month. In the fall, she
        accepts a full-time position in Cardinal, close to her Uncle
        Excide's house.

1930   Roy returns to Saint-Boniface to teach at the Académie
        Provencher, an all-boys' school. The principal assigns her
        the immigrant children. While living at home during the
        1930s and helping support her mother and her ailing sister,
        Clémence, she joins a troupe of amateur actors who pres-
        ent variety shows at various French-speaking parishes in
        Manitoba. Roy also performs with a more professional
        group of actors, Le Cercle Molière.

1937   To earn money for Europe, Roy takes a summer job teach-
        ing children on an isolated island in northern Manitoba,

Petite-Poule-d'Eau. This experience evolves into her second novel, *Where Nests the Water Hen*. Quitting her job during the Depression, Roy leaves Saint-Boniface in the fall to travel and study drama in France and in England.

1938   Roy returns to London, where she has a brief love affair with Stephen, an undercover agent for a Ukrainian independence movement. She meets Esther and Father Perfect, whose home in Epping Forest provides the refuge that fosters Gabrielle's serious attempts at writing. Roy's first articles get published in Paris, Winnipeg, and Montreal. Owing to a medical condition, her acting aspirations end.

1939   Five months before the start of World War II, she arrives back in Canada, choosing not to return to Saint-Boniface but to pursue a writing career in Montreal. During 1939–45, she publishes over one hundred newspaper columns, articles, and short stories; some fifty pieces by Roy appear in *Le bulletin des agriculteurs*. Roy travels extensively in Canada. In 1939, the editors of *La revue moderne* name Roy's short story "La conversion des O'Connor" best story of the year.

1943   Gabrielle's mother, Mélina, dies at the age of seventy-six. Seeking solace, Gabrielle begins to exchange letters with her sister Bernadette, a cloistered nun. Their correspondence continues until Bernadette's death in 1970.

1945   Gérard Dagenais at Éditions Pascal publishes *The Tin Flute* in Montreal; its success is immediate. The novel will eventually be translated into more than twelve languages.

1946   *The Tin Flute* wins Gabrielle the Médaille Richelieu from the Académie française and the Médaille "Feu qui dure" from the Académie canadienne-française.

1947   A landmark year: *The Tin Flute* is chosen by the Literary Guild of America as its May Book of the Month and wins the Governor General's Award; Roy becomes the first female member of the Royal Society of Canada when she is awarded the Lorne Pierce Medal; and a major Hollywood studio purchases film rights for *The Tin Flute* in June for $75,000. On a summer visit to Saint-Boniface, Roy meets

Dr. Marcel Carbotte; they marry on 26 August and leave for a three-year stay in France, where Marcel pursues medical studies. In November, Gabrielle wins the prestigious Prix Femina in Paris, the first Canadian ever so honoured. Her travels include time with the Perfects in England. There, some ten years after starting her writing career at that cottage, she suspends work on *The Cashier* and begins writing *Where Nests the Water Hen*.

1950   In June, Marcel and Gabrielle return to Canada and move to Ville LaSalle, a suburb of Montreal. *Where Nests the Water Hen* is published. Her personal favourite, the book eventually becomes a teaching text in many English and French schools but does not enjoy great popularity outside Canada. The Canadian Women's Press Club names Gabrielle "Woman of the Year."

1952   Gabrielle and Marcel move to Quebec City, where Gabrielle spends the rest of her life.

1954   *The Cashier* is published.

1955   *Street of Riches* is published.

1956   Quebec's Saint-Jean Baptiste Society awards Gabrielle its Prix Duvernay for her work. Joseph, the eldest Roy sibling, dies in Dollard, Saskatchewan, one of the many villages Roy's father founded in western Canada during his years as a settlement agent.

1957   Gabrielle travels with artist René Richard (the inspiration for Pierre Cadorai in *The Hidden Mountain*) and his wife to the southern United States. Gabrielle and Marcel purchase a cottage at Petite-Rivière-Saint-François, about sixty-five miles north of Quebec City, where they spend their summers. The English translation of *Street of Riches* earns Roy her second Governor General's Award.

1961   Roy's brother Germain dies in a car accident. Roy travels to Ungava, in northern Quebec, Vienna, and Greece. *The Hidden Mountain* is published.

1964   Gabrielle spends two weeks in Arizona with Anna and her family. Anna dies on 19 January.

1965   Gabrielle's sisters Bernadette and Clémence arrive in Petite-Rivière-Saint-François for a much-anticipated summer visit with Marcel and Gabrielle.

1966   *The Road Past Altamont* is published.

1967   *Man and His World* is published, a collection of photographs commissioned by the Canadian government to celebrate the Montreal Expo. Roy writes the introductory essay, "Terre des hommes." She is named a Companion of the Order of Canada.

1968   Roy receives an honorary Doctorate ès lettres from Laval University and wins the Canada Council Medal for her work.

1970   Roy goes to Saint-Boniface to comfort the ailing Bernadette, who dies in May. *Windflower* is published. Gabrielle signs an agreement with the National Film Board, which produces a multimedia presentation in French and English based on *Where Nests the Water Hen* — "Of Many People" / "Un siècle d'hommes" — for Manitoba's centennial celebrations.

1971   The Quebec government honours Roy with the Prix David for her work. Rodolphe, Gabrielle's ne'er-do-well brother, dies an alcoholic at the age of seventy-two.

1972   *Enchanted Summer*, inspired by Bernadette, is published.

1975   *Garden in the Wind* is published. The American Association of Teachers of French makes Roy an honorary member.

1976   *Ma vache Bossie*, a children's story, is published. In March, the Toronto Board of Education honours Roy by naming a French elementary school the École Publique Gabrielle Roy.

1977   *Children of My Heart* is published. Roy's works begin to appear in paperback.

1978   Roy wins the Prix Molson from the Canada Council. *The Fragile Lights of Earth*, a collection of her earlier journalistic works and essays from 1942–70, is published. *Children of My Heart* earns Roy her third Governor General's Award.

1979   *Courte-queue*, a children's story, is published.

1980   The Conseil des arts au Canada honours *Courte-queue* with its Prix de littérature de jeunesse.

1982   *De quoi t'ennuies-tu, Eveline?* is published.

1983   On 13 July, Gabrielle Roy dies of heart failure at the age of seventy-four in Quebec City. At the time of her death, the film version of *The Tin Flute* premieres and wins high praise at the Moscow Film Festival.

1984   Roy's autobiography, *Enchantment and Sorrow*, is published.

1986   *L'espagnole et la pékinoise*, Roy's third children's story, is published. The National Film Board produces *The Old Man and the Child*, a feature film based on a story from *The Road Past Altamont*.

1988   *Letters to Bernadette* is published, a collection of Gabrielle's letters to her beloved sister from 1943 to 1970.

1989   Dr. Marcel Carbotte dies at the age of seventy-five.

WORKS CONSULTED

Bednarski, Betty. "To Hold Happiness in One Hand, Gabrielle Roy's Autobiography." Rev. of *Enchantment and Sorrow*. *Antigonish Review* 76 (1989): 25–33.

Cameron, David. "Gabrielle Roy: A Bird in the Prison Window." *Conversations with Canadian Novelists — 2*. Toronto: Macmillan, 1973. 128–45.

Cobb, David. " 'I have, I think, a grateful heart.' " *Canadian* [*Toronto Star*] 1 May 1976: 10–14.

Dagenais, Gérard. "Nos écrivains et le français." *La presse* 16 Apr. 1966.

Delson-Karan, Myrna. "The Last Interview: Gabrielle Roy." *Quebec Studies* 4 (1986): 194–205.

Dicakson, Tony. "Gabrielle Roy's Own Story Recalled by Sister Here." *Winnipeg Tribune* 1 Mar. 1947: 13.

Duncan, Dorothy. "Le triomphe de Gabrielle." *Maclean's* 15 Apr. 1947: 23, 51, 54.

"Gabrielle Roy humiliée." *Le devoir* 28 Apr. 1978: 19.

Gagné, Marc. *Visages de Gabrielle Roy, l'oeuvre et l'écrivain*. Montréal: Beauchemin, 1973.

Grosskurth, Phyllis. *Gabrielle Roy*. Canadian Writers and Their Works. Ed. William French. Toronto: Forum, 1969.

Hesse, M.G. *Gabrielle Roy*. Twayne's World Authors Series 726. Boston: Twayne, 1984.

Hind-Smith, Joan. *Three Voices: The Lives of Margaret Laurence, Gabrielle Roy, Frederick Philip Grove*. Toronto: Clarke, 1975.

Labonté, René. "Gabrielle Roy, journaliste, au fil de ses reportages (1939–1945)." *Studies in Canadian Literature* 7 (1982): 90–108.

Lewis, Paula Gilbert. "Feminism and Traditionalism in the Early Short Stories of Gabrielle Roy." *Traditionalism, Nationalism, and Feminism: Women Writers of Quebec*. Ed. Paula Gilbert Lewis. Contributions in Women's Studies 53. Westport, CT: Greenwood, 1985. 27–35.

———. "The Last of the Great Storytellers: A Visit with Gabrielle Roy." *French Review* 55 (1981): 207–15.

Manitoba Heritage Council. *Gabrielle Roy: The Manitoba Years*. Winnipeg: Manitoba Heritage Council, 1991.

Marshall, Joyce. "Gabrielle Roy 1909–1983." *Antigonish Review* 55 (1983): 35–46.

Mitcham, Allison. *The Literary Achievement of Gabrielle Roy*. Fredericton, NB: York, 1983.

———. "Roy's West." *Canadian Literature* 88 (1981): 161–63.

Murphy, John J. "Visit with Gabrielle Roy." *Thought* [Fordham U] 38 (1963): 447–55.

Ricard, François. "Le cercle enfin uni des hommes: hommage à Gabrielle Roy pour sa trentième année de création littéraire." *Liberté* 109 (1976): 59–78.

——— . *Gabrielle Roy.* Montréal: Fides, 1975.

——— . *Inventaire des archives personnelles de Gabrielle Roy conservées à la Bibliothèque nationale du Canada.* Montréal: Boréal, 1992.

——— . "La métamorphose d'un écrivain: essai biographique." *Études littéraires* 17 (1984): 441–55.

Ringuet. "Conversation avec Gabrielle Roy." *La revue populaire* Oct. 1951: 4.

Roy, Gabrielle. "Après trois cents ans." *Le bulletin des agriculteurs* 37 (1941): 9, 37–39.

——— . *The Cashier.* Trans. Harry Binsse. Toronto: McClelland, 1955. Trans. of *Alexandre Chenevert.* Montréal: Beauchemin, 1954.

——— . "Chapeau bas: réminiscences de la vie théâtrale et musicale du Manitoba français." *Les cahiers d'histoire de la Société historique de Saint-Boniface.* Saint-Boniface, MB: Éditions du Blé pour la Société historique de Saint-Boniface, 1980–85. 116–24.

——— . *Children of My Heart.* Trans. Alan Brown. Toronto: McClelland, 1979. Trans. of *Ces enfants de ma vie.* Montréal: Stanké, 1977.

——— . "La Conversion des O'Connor." *La revue moderne* 21.5 (1939): 4.

——— . *Courte-queue.* Montréal: Stanké, 1979.

——— . *De quoi t'ennuies-tu, Eveline? suivi de Ely! Ely! Ely!* Montréal: Boréal, 1984.

——— . *Enchanted Summer.* Trans. Joyce Marshall. Toronto: McClelland, 1976. Trans. of *Cet été qui chantait.* Québec: Éditions françaises, 1972.

——— . *Enchantment and Sorrow: The Autobiography of Gabrielle Roy.* Trans. Patricia Claxton. Toronto: Lester, 1987. Trans. of *La détresse et l'enchantement.* Montréal: Boréal, 1984.

——— . *L'espagnole et la pékinoise.* Montréal: Boréal Jeunesse, 1986.

——— . *The Fragile Lights of Earth: Articles and Memories 1942–1970.* Trans. Alan Brown. Toronto: McClelland, 1982. Trans. of *Fragiles lumières de la terre.* Montréal: Éditions Quinze, 1978.

——— . *Garden in the Wind.* Trans. Alan Brown. Toronto: McClelland, 1977. Trans. of *Un jardin au bout du monde.* Montréal: Beauchemin, 1975.

——— . *The Hidden Mountain.* Trans. Harry Binsse. Toronto: McClelland, 1962. Trans. of *La montagne secrète.* Montréal: Beauchemin, 1961.

——— . Introduction. *Man and His World.* By Pavel Eisner. Photographs by Faber. Montréal: Canadian Corporation for the 1967 World Exhibition, 1967. Rpt. in *Fragile Lights* 193–222.

——— . *Letters to Bernadette.* Trans. Patricia Claxton. Montréal: Lester, 1990. Trans. of *Ma chère petite soeur: lettres à Bernadette 1943–1970.* Ed. François Ricard. Montréal: Boréal, 1988.

——— . "Lettre de Gabrielle Roy à ses amis de l'ALCQ." *Studies in Canadian Literature* 4 (1979): 101–04.

——— . *Ma vache Bossie.* Montréal: Leméac, 1976.

——— . *The Road Past Altamont.* Trans. Joyce Marshall. New York: Harcourt, 1966. Trans. of *La route d'Altamont.* Montréal: HMH, 1966.

——— . *Street of Riches.* Trans. Harry Binsse. Lincoln: U of Nebraska P, 1993. Trans. of *Rue Deschambault.* Montréal: Beauchemin, 1955.

————. *The Tin Flute*. Trans. Hannah Josephson. Toronto: McClelland, 1969. Trans. of *Bonheur d'occasion*. Montréal: Pascal, 1945.

————. *Where Nests the Water Hen*. Trans. Harry Binsse. Toronto: McClelland, 1986. Trans. of *La petite poule d'eau*. Montréal: Beauchemin, 1950.

————. *Windflower*. Trans. Joyce Marshall. Toronto: McClelland, 1970. Trans. of *La rivière sans repos*. Montréal: Beauchemin, 1970.

Scott, Gail. "A Passionate Heritage at Home in Quebec." *Globe and Mail* 8 Oct. 1977: 33.

Socken, Paul G. "Gabrielle Roy: An Annotated Bibliography." *The Annotated Bibliography of Canada's Major Authors*. Ed. Robert Lecker and Jack David. Vol. 1. Downsview, ON: ECW, 1979. 213–61.

————. "In Memoriam: Gabrielle Roy (1909–1983)." *Canadian Modern Language Review/Revue canadienne des langues vivantes* 40 (1983): 105–10.

————. *Myth and Morality in «Alexandre Chenevert» by Gabrielle Roy*. European University Studies, Series 13: French Language and Literature. Frankfurt am Main: Lang, 1987.

Whitfield, Agnès. "Relire Gabrielle Roy, écrivaine." *Queen's Quarterly* 97 (1990): 53–66.

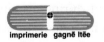

imprimerie   gagné ltēe

PRINTED IN CANADA